Alfie's Woods

By

Alfie Dog

with a little help from

Rosemary J. Kind

Printed in the United Kingdom

First Printing in paperback, 2013 Alfie Dog Limited

The author can be found at: authors@alfiedog.com

Cover image: Katie Stewart, Magic Owl Designs

ISBN 978-1-909894-13-6

Published by
Alfie Dog Limited
Rose Bank, Norton Lindsey,
Warwickshire, CV35 8JQ
Tel: 07712 647754

DEDICATION

To

the many creatures of the woodlands behind our house in Belgium who provided the inspiration for the characters in this story

and

To

the owners of the woodlands who allowed us to enjoy their land. We will always have the very happiest memories of the times we spent in those woods.

Alfie Dog & Rosemary J. Kind

INTRODUCTION

It all began with an acorn, as many things do. In my case, it was eating rather than planting the acorn that kicked things off. I liked it. Actually, I liked it quite a lot and wanted another and then some more.

You might think I'm vegetarian, but I'm not. Acorns as it turned out were bad for me, but I wouldn't have known that from the smell. They smelled divine. I'm a red blooded omnivorous dog. That means I eat anything and I do in fact mean anything. I'll try a shoe or a bit of wood, a tennis ball or an old rag and all with equal enthusiasm. I do have a penchant for cat poo and horse manure, but I discovered that next to the food I steal from the Boss's plate, I like acorns best.

I'm Alfie and I'm an Entlebucher. I live with the Boss who is basically the person who does all the chores for me, in return for a bit of love and attention. It's not a bad system. If you'd like to, you can come with me and be part of the world that is my woods. Although, I don't think the Boss will stretch to doing your chores as well, so it may help if you bring a sandwich or two to keep you going.

I've got some friends I'd like you to meet and a few scrapes to get us into. So come on, what are you waiting for? Let's go.

CHAPTER 1
THE ACORNS

Breakfast is such a special time of day. It isn't called 'break fast' for nothing and I'm always ready to embrace the idea of eating. I stretch my tongue to get the final crumbs from the corners of my mouth; then I have another quick look in my bowl, in case I've missed anything. The bowl is quite deep and I tend to wipe the edges with my ears, but I can soon sort that out. I always hope that some extra breakfast might have appeared whilst I'm not looking, but except for the little bone pattern on the bottom of my bowl, sad to say it's always empty, licked clean and likely to remain that way until the next meal time. I've been told if I watch my figure while I'm young I'll reap the benefits later, but I don't buy that idea. I think it's a cost saving initiative.

One cold morning, just as I was finishing breakfast, I was about to feel disappointed about my empty bowl, when the doorbell rang. Given it was still only eight in the morning it was very exciting that someone was already calling for me, so I skipped to the front door. I was at the stage where I skipped everywhere and regularly tripped over in the process. I couldn't wait to see who was at the door, so I put that extra bit of bounce into my skip, the one I save for unexpected and special occasions. I learned the trick of opening the front door as soon as I was big enough to reach the handle. It's one of those useful skills that every freedom-loving dog needs to learn. As education goes, it's right up there with mapping the route of the central heating pipes so you can always find a warm patch of floor to lie on.

When I opened the front door, it turned out to be a very unexpected occasion indeed. I stopped skipping or wagging my tail. There in front of me stood the police badger. Now badgers can look serious at the best of times, their white stripe seems to have that effect. Just the sight of them is enough to make me start thinking something really bad has happened. Well in this case it wasn't so much that it had happened, it was more that it was about to happen and it was about to happen to me. There Badger was, wearing his helmet, with its badge gleaming and his perfectly pressed uniform, making him look very important.

He cleared his throat and said in a gruff voice, "Good morning, I'm PC Badger of the Woodland Police. Can you tell me what you were doing yesterday afternoon?"

Badger's brow went all wrinkly as he took his pencil from his top pocket and held it poised above his notebook. Then he just looked at me, wiggling his nose, waiting for me to answer.

I'd been practising wiggling my nose, but now didn't seem like the time to do it in reply. I gulped. I knew the police were the ones I should go to if I needed help, but this time seemed different. I've watched television programmes with police in them, but this was the real thing. It's a bit different meeting a real police officer rather than having a daydream about some big crime in which the police ask me questions. In my daydreams, I'm the star of the show. I always imagine a bit of a friendly chat and me giving them evidence that leads them to find some arch-criminal. This wasn't like that at all. Here we were, with Badger straight into the questions without me even having chance to introduce myself properly.

I stood there, moving from paw to paw, but he was still staring at me. I scratched my head with my back leg and said, "Well I went for a walk in the woods at the back of our house, sir." I thought calling Badger 'sir' seemed appropriate somehow. I've seen it in films and I didn't know what else to say. The only comfort I had was that Badger hadn't said that bit about 'anything you say may be taken down and given in evidence'. As he wrote on his notepad, I got that sinking feeling that warnings like that may not apply in the Woodland Police and that just possibly I had been watching the wrong type of films.

"I have a report here from the Security Buzzard, saying that he saw you in the vicinity of the path from the wood to the bridleway at about 3.45pm."

Being totally unaware that I'd done anything wrong, never having heard of a 'Security Buzzard' and not connecting that this might in some way be a bad thing, I said "What does 'vicinity' mean?"

"The general area." He sighed heavily and chewed the end of his pencil. "You were in the general area of the footpath."

"Yes, sir, I was, but I think it may have been nearer to 3.30pm."

As PC Badger glared at me over his notebook, I got goose bumps and could feel my hair sticking out in all directions.

"And what were you 'doing' while you were there at 3.30pm?" I detected a slight note of sarcasm in his tone. Then he screwed his eyes up as if to see me better.

"I was just out for a walk." My voice was a high-pitched squeak and I wondered for a minute who was talking.

"Were you alone?" He was scribbling furiously as I

spoke.

"No," I squeaked.

"And who were you with, Dog?"

No one calls me by my surname. The way PC Badger was talking to me, made me realise that this was not good news. "I was with the Boss."

PC Badger flipped back several pages in his notebook. "Did you see any acorns while you were out?"

"No," I said, trying to cross my paws without him seeing.

"I have a report here from Squirrel to say that some of her acorns have been stolen. Do you know anything about it, Dog?"

"Who's Squirrel and what's a Security Buzzard?" I squeaked.

PC Badger didn't answer my questions. "I shall be back with some papers that let me search your house, young Dog, so if there is anything else that you want to tell me, now would be a good time."

"No," I said in a very small voice.

As I closed the door, my heart was pounding. I needed to act quickly, but I had no idea what to do. Should I eat the evidence before PC Badger came back? Should I return the acorns to Squirrel's store and see if she would withdraw her complaint? Should I drop all pretence that dogs only say 'woof' and explain the problem to the Boss?

I didn't know the acorns already belonged to someone. I thought they'd buried themselves. I couldn't return the whole stash to Squirrel. I'd already eaten some. Admittedly, since then I hadn't been feeling well, but I had no idea that the acorns might be responsible for that. I wondered if I could make up the shortfall in dog biscuits.

Given I was a young puppy and still getting the hang of

things, would PC Badger let me off if I explained to him what really happened? Perhaps he could give me a bit of a telling off and Squirrel would be happy. At least I'd know for next time. There was no need to send me to prison. I wasn't really a bad dog. I just didn't understand.

That night I tossed and turned in my basket, feeling every wrinkle of my blanket. What should I do about the acorns? What would I do if they sent me to prison? Was I going to spend the rest of my life behind bars? Mum told me so many stories about the sorts of houses that young puppies lived in, but nowhere did she mention prison. I gulped and rolled over again. I'd been so lucky to arrive in a home that was nearly perfect. I'd be very sad if I had to leave it so soon.

Then there was a hand on my collar. I thrashed around with my paws, pushing and kicking as they chained me to the wall of my cell ready to torture me.

"Alfie, Alfie, are you all right?"

I opened my eyes and saw a face staring at me. I backed further into the corner of my bed, away from the face. Then I realised it was the Boss looking down at me, gently stroking my head. I nestled up to her and began to relax. Then I saw my food bowl and sat up. They wouldn't have to torture me. They could just stop feeding me. How is a dog to get any sleep after a thought like that? She rubbed my tummy and very slowly I drifted back to sleep.

The next thing I knew Police Badger was arresting me and the Boss wouldn't rescue me. Fortunately, I woke up again and wished more than anything that I was still back with my brothers and sisters, snuggled up to Mum. I was sure she would know what to do.

I snuggled deeper into my bed and put my paws around my cushion for comfort. I could be brave; I would be just fine. I got out of bed to find my cuddly toy and then nestled right into the corner of my bed with my cushion and my blanket just as close as I could get them. The Boss would rescue me, of course she would. Then I ran through the things I could do to sort the problem out, just in case I'd missed one.

I could try to convince PC Badger that it wasn't me. I could admit to having been there, but maybe I could persuade him that the Boss stole the acorns. Mum wouldn't be very proud of me if I did that. She probably wouldn't be very proud of me if I ended up in prison either. Maybe fibbing is better than being in prison. I don't actually know what a Security Buzzard is, so that plan might not work. I was the one with my nose stuck in the ground and my paws slinging dirt in all directions. I sat up and looked at my claws, which is difficult to do in the dark. I decided the first thing I needed to do in the morning was give them a good scrub to get rid of the rest of the dirt.

As soon as I went outside after breakfast, I had a quick look to make sure there was no one in my patch of garden. I looked under the bushes and then made sure that there was nobody standing looking out of any of the windows of the house. Then as quickly as my paws would go, I started digging. I dug and dug until I uncovered all the acorns.

"Hey, what do you think you're doing?" A rabbit poked up, spluttering soil out of his mouth.

"I… well, I'm Alfie." I looked quizzically at the rabbit with his slicked back hair.

"And I'm Rabbit, but I didn't want to be covered in soil. I was just trying to come up for air." His nose and ears both twitched as he spoke.

"I'm pleased to meet you. I was just… I'm sorry. I didn't know you were there."

Rabbit grinned. "Not like me then, I'd have done it deliberately if I knew you were there. I have great fun, though I must admit to getting into the odd bit of bother. Well I never knew all these acorns were buried here."

I felt myself blushing. "I'm already in a bit of bother," I said, without thinking. "I was just about to have one for breakfast, would you like one."

"Steady on there. Aren't they supposed to be toxic for dogs?"

"What's toxic?" I lifted an acorn towards my nose and sniffed.

"Poisonous. Bad for you. Make you ill. I don't think you should eat them."

My shoulders slumped. "That might explain the stomach ache then. If I can't eat them, what else am I going to do?"

"I don't know why you're trying to get rid of them, but this seems like a fun game. See that pond over there?"

I nodded as I looked at the gnome sitting fishing in the neighbouring garden.

"Let's see who can throw the most into the pond. A point for each one."

I took the first turn and threw short.

Rabbit threw his first acorn and made a nice splash. After half an hour or so with Rabbit very much in the lead, I was having a great time and had completely forgotten about PC Badger.

Rabbit threw the last acorn and hit the centre of the pond. "I win. Anyway, must dash. Perhaps I'll see you later." And with that he'd gone.

As I went back towards the house, I suddenly hoped that PC Badger didn't know Rabbit and wasn't going to hear about our little game.

There were still one or two acorns on the ground, but I hoped that the oak tree nearby would make it look as though the few remaining acorns should have been there. I washed my paws, paying particular attention to the mud under my claws, until I was satisfied that no one could work out what my morning activity had been. If only I'd known they belonged to someone, but I didn't, at least not until it was too late.

I still had tummy ache from the ones I had eaten, but on top of that I felt a very unhappy puppy. I wasn't very proud of my behaviour. Now Rabbit might work out what I'd done too. There was no way I could go on living my life like this. I was going to confess.

Please don't misunderstand me. I wasn't going to see PC Badger. That would be a step too far, for a not very brave puppy. No, my plan was to see Squirrel, somehow she sounded nice and I thought she might understand. I didn't know what she looked like or where she lived, but I knew I needed to find her.

CHAPTER 2
IN SEARCH OF SQUIRREL

The Boss was busy, clearing up where I'd been sick from the acorns I had eaten earlier. I slipped out through the back gate to look for Squirrel. I didn't really notice the drizzle as I talked to myself for courage. I hadn't been into the woods on my own before. I was scared. I needed all the encouragement I could get.

"I know I'm looking for Squirrel and I think PC Badger said something about sleeping, but maybe she'll be awake. I don't know where to look. Where would I find a squirrel? What if I find her and she's asleep, but then I wouldn't know I'd found her if she wasn't awake. I wonder if she minds being woken up? I could wake her very gently. I suppose it might be frightening to be woken by a strange puppy; perhaps I'd better not do that."

Then I started practising what I was going to say. "It's like this Squirrel, I'm only twelve weeks old and I'm still learning how things work around here. No one explained to me that acorns might belong to somebody..." No, I needed to get the words right. "I really didn't mean to do something bad, I just didn't know. Oh, what am I going to tell her?"

"We must stop meeting like this. What are you going to tell who?" Rabbit bounced a bit as he spoke. He was carrying a bunch of carrots with a supermarket label attached to the tops. I thought better than to ask him where they were from as there was no supermarket nearby.

"Oh, hello. I was just looking for Squirrel."

"This isn't about all those acorns is it?" Rabbit bounced again, making me feel more nervous.

I looked down at my paws. "What acorns?"

"It is isn't it? You're the one who stole the acorns." Rabbit was grinning.

"No, I… well yes. Oh what am I going to do?"

"Well you sound like my sort of chap," he said, holding up the carrots. "I'm sure you meant no harm. Just a bit of fun hey? Dig them up from one place then bury them somewhere else. I don't suppose you were expecting the police to be involved for a few acorns. Still PC Badger's not so bad really, although he does a good line in telling off." Rabbit pulled himself up to his full height and tried to look stern. He wagged his finger at me as he said, "Now don't you go doing it again, young Alfie." He relaxed, "Ha ha, you'll be for it."

"I didn't mean any harm. Do you know where Squirrel lives?"

"Can't say that I do. Perhaps best not to mention our little game. Anyway, good luck old chap and I'll see you later." Then Rabbit bounced off back along the path.

Once he'd gone I was just as lost as I had been before. At a guess, Squirrel must live somewhere close to where I found the acorns. I went along the bridleway and looked up at each oak tree in turn, to see if any of them would give me a clue. I hoped there might be house names that said who lived where, but instead there were just the usual numbers. I'd have to try a different way. I sniffed. It wasn't a bunged-up nose sort of sniff, but a long, cool, getting a feel for the air type of sniff.

Being a hound, I can follow a scent quite easily and it's always fun to see where it leads. I sniffed at each tree as I went past. Perhaps I should start from the acorn stash. I was starting to feel a little more jolly and waved a paw in case this Security Buzzard that PC Badger mentioned was watching.

I was very careful not to eat any acorns accidentally. I was still feeling a bit ill, so it wasn't that difficult to resist. Once I sniffed the ground around the acorn stash I could pick up several scents, the main one being a reminder that I had spent quite some time digging there recently and that the Boss had been with me. Then I caught another more gentle smell, a smell that at first sniff was quite wonderful.

Oh my! I took a step backwards. Oh how beautiful. I guessed that scent was probably Squirrel. The smell gave the impression of something very delicate. I laughed out loud, I couldn't imagine that this was the smell that PC Badger would have left behind.

Finding Squirrel's scent reminded me of why I was there and all of a sudden, my courage vanished. There I was, nose to the ground, alternately sniffing nervously and saying, "I can be a brave puppy, I can be a brave puppy, I can be a brave puppy." I wasn't feeling like a brave puppy at all.

I was just on my third chant of "I can be a brave puppy," rather less to myself than I thought, when a small voice asked;

"Why do you need to be a brave puppy?"

I looked up from my sniffing and there in front of me was simply the most lovely, petite creature, with a stunning body of red hair, such dainty features and the most perfect bushy tail. My jaw dropped open. "I, well it's, what I mean is, perhaps…"

"Is something wrong?" Squirrel asked quickly climbing up the trunk of the nearest tree until she was just above my head.

I had just fallen in love, which I wasn't about to tell Squirrel. I couldn't think of anything wrong in the whole world. Instead, I lost all control of my brain and I poured out the whole story, not at all in the order that I had been practising it. I had been so determined to build up the picture of a poor innocent puppy who couldn't really be held responsible for such a dreadful crime, but it just didn't come out like that, not even a little bit.

"I did it. It was me. I'm guilty."

Squirrel dropped gracefully to the ground, then ran up onto another tree trunk until she was at the same height as me and asked, "What on earth are you talking about?"

"The acorns, I stole them. I'm sorry."

"Why don't we sit down and you can start from the beginning," Squirrel's little voice almost whispered in my ear. It sent the most wonderful shiver down my spine, so I sat down and tried to begin.

"I'm Alfie," was all I could say.

"Well, hello, Alfie. I'm Squirrel." She held out a tiny paw to shake mine. "Do you live near here?"

Then suddenly, I couldn't stop talking. "I moved into the house just along the bridleway about two weeks ago. I was ten weeks old and had just left my mum. The Boss is great, but I miss Mum. I had a brother and three sisters and we all snuggled up together when we were tired from playing. Now there's just me."

Squirrel moved a little closer and put her paw on mine.

"Oh, it's ok, I've got lots of toys and a really nice bed and I do get lots of love, but it can be a bit lonely." I had no idea why I was telling all this to an animal I'd only just met. There was something very special about Squirrel. "Anyway, I discovered that I really like the taste of acorns and when I was out walking I found a whole pile of them and I didn't know they belonged to anyone, so I ate one." I began to feel a little embarrassed as I explained. "Then the next day I picked a few up and carried them home. Then a few more and well that was how it all happened really. I'm so very sorry. I would give them all back, but the problem is that when PC Badger called, I was very scared and so I had a game with Rabbit and threw them in next door's pond. The ones I ate made me feel quite poorly. I feel very ashamed of myself, but it feels good to tell the truth."

Squirrel just gave me a little hug. "Alfie, I think you are quite wonderful. You have been so brave and honest that I forgive you completely. With the weather warming up, I'd gone for a little walk to check on supplies and make sure everything was in order, before going back to sleep. When I found some of my acorns missing, I felt I had no choice but to talk to PC Badger. I nearly ran out last winter and I didn't want it to happen again. I worked very hard all through the autumn to make sure I would have enough food. If I'd known that it was a mistake and that it was you, Alfie, I would never have gone to see Badger." She grinned. "I might have known Rabbit would be involved somewhere."

I sat and looked at her thinking how amazing she was. "It wasn't really Rabbit's fault. I'd already taken them by then. I did wonder if I could persuade PC Badger that although I was there, it was really the Boss doing the digging, but I don't really like being dishonest."

"Oh, Alfie," said Squirrel with tears in her eyes from laughing. "I don't think you would have confused PC Badger that easily, but I'd have liked to see you try."

I was starting to feel a lot better. "What's a Security Buzzard?"

"The Security Buzzard is like all the cameras that people put around their towns, but for the animal world. He keeps watch on all the goings on in the forest and then reports back to PC Badger. I really don't think he would get confused between a human and a wobbly puppy." Squirrel was still laughing.

"I don't suppose he needs glasses does he?"

Squirrel wiped her eyes. "No, I really don't think he does."

"Squirrel, I'll do anything to make amends. Would it help if I save some of my dog biscuits and bring them to you?" I was desperately crossing the claws on one paw as I said it.

"Squirrels don't eat dog biscuits," said Squirrel kindly.

I breathed a sigh of relief. I wasn't really sure I was capable of not eating a dog biscuit so that I could save it for Squirrel. "The boss puts food out for the birds every day, including peanuts, would you like to come to our garden to eat some?" I felt shy as I asked her.

"That would be lovely, but first I need to see PC Badger and tell him that everything is sorted out and he doesn't need to bother you again."

I yawned. "I'm sorry, Squirrel. I didn't sleep well for worrying. I feel very, very tired. I think I may have to go home and take a nap."

"I have that problem at this time of year. Sometimes I can sleep for days."

"You will come for elevenses won't you?"

"Yes, of course I will. I should rather like to see your garden anyway." Then she waved her paw as I trotted unsteadily down the path. I shall be glad when I'm bigger and more stable on my feet. It's one of the hardest things about being so young, that and not knowing acorns might belong to someone.

CHAPTER 3
HEDGEHOG RECAPTURED

One bright, crisp day, when the weather was warming up again, the Boss took me for a walk on a completely different route. There were so many new sights and sounds to learn and remember. I felt as though I was the luckiest puppy in the world. I saw my first snowdrop and daffodil and thought wow! Where did they come from?

I was sniffing the air and there it was, the nutty smell of acorns. This wasn't the very faint smell of a single acorn, but the deep intoxicating scent of lots of acorns. My tummy was feeling much better, and I was back to thinking that they were simply the most wonderful of foods, but I remembered what Rabbit had said and decided I'd better not eat any.

"Acorns! Wow!"

"Pardon?" said the Boss.

Oh bother, talking was one of the things Mum warned me not to do. I'm not supposed to give away that I can talk quite that easily. I cleared my throat, "Acchoo, woowfff," with more of a 'woof' than the 'wow'.

Then I realised I'd replied when someone said 'pardon?' There was a risk the Boss would work out I could understand, but she's quite convinced that I can understand every word she says anyway and of course I can, when I want to.

I snuffled my nose slightly and found that the smell was coming from… well everywhere. I looked around me, there they were, lots and lots of acorns. These ones weren't even buried. They couldn't possibly have belonged to anyone. I was so excited and couldn't wait to tell Squirrel. Despite the fact that I knew they tasted better than almost anything, I didn't eat a single one. I wanted to save them all for her and quite apart from anything else, I didn't want to be ill.

Later, on my own, when I plucked up the courage to go into the wood to find Squirrel, the sun was filtering through the trees making dancing patterns between the branches. I could hear the steady rhythm of a helicopter circling overhead and wondered what it was doing. I felt nervous as I went to knock on the oak tree that was Squirrel's door. I was worried in case she didn't want to see me and I wasn't even sure whether she'd be awake. She was busy spring-cleaning and was delighted to have some company for an excuse to stop work.

Before I had any opportunity to tell Squirrel of my exciting find, she put down her little broom and shrieked, "Why, Alfie you've grown so much. You're becoming such a handsome dog."

I could feel my face going red. I hadn't noticed how much I was changing.

"Turn around so that I can see all of you."

I felt embarrassed, but did as she asked.

"Can I have a ride on your back?"

As we set off a mole ran past shouting. "There's a prisoner escaped. There's a prisoner escaped."

"Oh my, oh dear," Squirrel cried. "You'd best take me home, Alfie."

"How exciting, can't we join the hunt. Do you think that's what the helicopter's out for?" I asked Squirrel.

"I suppose so. Perhaps we should stay indoors for safety."

"Are prisoners very dangerous?" I was fascinated.

"I don't know. Here, we're home. Will you come in Alfie?"

I hesitated. "Perhaps I'd better be getting back."

"You will go back won't you? You aren't going to try to find the prisoner are you? You take care. See you later." Squirrel waved.

"Oh, Squirrel, I almost forgot. I've found you lots and lots of acorns. I'll show you tomorrow."

"Alfie, you are lovely. Thank you."

I waved a paw as she went inside.

Suddenly Rabbit appeared from nowhere. "How's it hanging, dude?"

"Pardon?"

"I don't even sound convincing do I? Oh well it was worth a try. What are you doing?" Rabbit said as he sat down next to me. "I was about to join the search for the prisoner. Do you want to come?" Without waiting for my reply he was up and heading towards the middle of the wood.

I got up and started to follow Rabbit.

"Wait for me," I panted. "What sort of prisoner is it? Is he dangerous?"

"Oh they're all dangerous. That's the fun of it." As the undergrowth thickened, Rabbit slowed down a little.

I could feel my heart pounding. "What are we looking for?" I whispered.

"Evidence," whispered Rabbit looking smug.

We crept along. I kept looking around me but couldn't see anything that might be evidence. There was a crackle. "What was that?" I hissed nervously.

"A twig," hissed back Rabbit in an exaggerated way.

We inched forwards, slowly feeling our way through

the undergrowth, when all of a sudden Rabbit turned around and shouted, "Boo."

I jumped and let out a whimper. "Rabbit! That wasn't fair."

Then he darted through a gap in the undergrowth and out into an open area.

I could see quite a crowd of animals ahead of us as I struggled to keep up. Then he wasn't there anymore and I'd no idea whether he'd disappeared down a hole or into the crowd.

"Rabbit. Rabbit. Where are you?" But there was no reply.

I carried on following the crowd of animals towards the middle of the wood, presuming they were taking part in the search.

"Not you again, laddie." From the badge he was wearing I realised this was the Security Buzzard.

Hardly the warmest of greetings. I'd prefer something like, "Alfie old chap, good to see you again," but I suppose not everyone is that friendly.

"Where do you think you're going?" The Security Buzzard really looked very serious.

"I've no idea. I was following Rabbit. I just thought I'd see where everyone else was going."

"Run along home, laddie," said Buzzard. "That's a meeting of the Woodland Council and you aren't on my list of members."

"I thought they were looking for the prisoner." I wandered off with my tail between my legs wondering how Rabbit got through without being stopped. As I walked, I kept looking over my shoulder and then looking at the ground for clues, but nothing seemed unusual. I went to call on Squirrel to see if she could tell me what the

Woodland Council was. She was sitting on a piece of wood, reading a book of acorn recipes.

She smiled. "Apparently it's Hedgehog who's escaped. I saw Rabbit's mum looking for Rabbit just after you left earlier. I don't think Hedgehog's really dangerous. That's why I came back out into the sunshine."

"Squirrel, what's the Woodland Council?"

"Well," she began, putting in her bookmark and carefully closing the page. "There's a council of the woodland animals with representatives for each area of the forest."

"Yes, but what do they do."

"I was getting to that. Now just be patient and I'll explain it all. They meet each season to sort forest business and on other occasions in an emergency. Despite the escaped hedgehog loose in the woods, this is the scheduled spring meeting. If it's still taking place it proves that there can't be much risk from the prisoner. Perhaps we could go to see those acorns after all."

"Right," I said, wanting to ask more questions about the helicopter and Hedgehog. "What else do the Woodland Council talk about?" What I really wanted to know was why Hedgehog was in prison. I was picturing a nasty animal causing all sorts of trouble. The picture I'd seen in the nature book at home had looked so cute, so this didn't fit with the image I had of hedgehogs in the slightest, except for the spines, but even they didn't look all that fearsome.

"At this time of year," said Squirrel, answering the question about the Woodland Council, "they have to decide which animals will be allowed to build new houses."

"How do the moles get away with all their tunnelling? I keep falling down their holes in the garden."

"That's all underground, so it's covered by some loop-hole in the regulations."

"Perhaps it should be a mole-hole in the regulations, and not a loop-hole." I kicked a stone without really thinking about it.

"Is something wrong?" Squirrel asked me.

"Not exactly. It was just something I was thinking about. Let's go to see those acorns." As we went I wondered if the Council would have to give permission to build a den. It was just an idea. Perhaps I should discuss it with Squirrel.

When Squirrel called round the following morning, I was feeling sleepy. I was stretched out on the patio with half an eye open for her arrival.

"Are you growing again?"

I yawned. "I didn't sleep very well last night."

"Oh dear, you weren't worrying about Hedgehog were you? Because if you were, I've got some good news."

"Hedgehog? Oh, no." I didn't know where to start. "I spent all night thinking about the Woodland Council and my den."

"Alfie, I don't know what you're talking about. Start at the beginning."

"Sorry." I wandered to the bird table to see if there were any stray crumbs. "I want to build a den. Rabbit seemed to think we could just do it."

"Oh, Alfie, how exciting." She clasped her tiny paws in front of her.

"I saw a tree with lots of sticks round it, when I was in the woods the other day and I suddenly thought; I could do a lot with a few sticks. That's when I had the idea for a den. I don't want it to be just any old den. I want it to be really special and then we can take some of the nuts there and eat them together."

"I could make some little curtains for the windows." Squirrel's face was beaming.

"Yes, but then you told me about the Woodland Council so I would probably need to ask them if I could build it."

"You mean you weren't going to build it in the garden?"

"No. I could be found too easily there."

"Then you're right. Whatever Rabbit might think, you will need permission, but I'll help you. It won't be a problem."

I brightened up immediately. Squirrel was always so positive. "I suppose it means I can't start building yet."

"Oh cheer up, Alfie." She threw some bird seed down to me. "There's another meeting soon. Spring is such a busy building time for the animals. We've got plenty of time to get the drawings done properly and the cost of the building worked out."

"I haven't got much money either. Whenever I get my pocket money I seem to spend it and then there isn't any left."

"You are a sad case today." Squirrel laughed. "I can help you open a savings account with the Woodland Bank and then when you get your pocket money you can put it in there and not spend it. You'll get interest on the money that stays there too, so it'll grow faster."

Squirrel always knew what to do, though I had absolutely no idea what interest was and why it meant that money would grow. Then I suddenly remembered, "What did you say about Hedgehog?"

"Oh, you're never going to believe it." Squirrel sounded excited and she came down to sit on the ground next to me. "Apparently, he walked up to one of the brushes that the stoats were using to clear up after the Woodland Council last night, thinking it was another hedgehog and asked if it could help him hide. He's short sighted and hadn't got his glasses on. The brush looked like the spines on a hedgehog. Well the stoats set the alarm off straight away and PC Badger was round in no time and rearrested him."

"Hedgehog looks so sweet. It's hard to think of him as a hardened criminal."

"Oh, he can be quite a prickly character," said Squirrel.

Since talking to Squirrel, I couldn't stop thinking about Hedgehog. I really found it hard to believe that such a lovely looking animal could be a criminal. I wanted to visit him and see what he was really like.

The first problem was that I didn't know where to find the Woodland Prison. I certainly didn't want to tell the Boss where I was going, as I didn't think she'd be too pleased. I wasn't really sure I wanted to ask Squirrel either, as she might have tried to stop me. Rabbit might have known, but I didn't want to ask him in case he wanted to come with me. Somehow I'd find a different way to get directions.

Squirrel said Hedgehog had been found guilty of money laundering, but how could accidentally leaving your money in your pocket, when you put it in the washing machine, be a crime? If leaving things in pockets were a crime, then the prisons would be constantly full of animals. I would have thought I should feel sorry for him if he lost some money whilst doing the laundry.

CHAPTER 4
TIGERS AND WILD BOAR

The next day I saw PC Badger.

"Good morning, Alfie." Badger sounded more kindly than before.

"Morning, PC Badger, sir." Then I added, "Where's the Woodland Prison?"

"Good heavens, young Alfie, what on earth are you thinking of doing this time?" Badger pulled himself up a little straighter.

"Oh no, sir, I was just wondering if I could visit Hedgehog. That was all."

Badger looked more surprised than if I'd said I was planning to steal all the acorns I could find. He didn't seem keen to tell me the answer. "Now what would you be wanting with that old reprobate?"

I had no idea what a 'reprobate' was and assumed it was a type of hedgehog. "I just thought he might like to have a visitor. It can't be much fun being stuck in prison."

"Prison isn't meant to be fun, young Alfie. It's meant as a punishment and of course to protect the rest of the woodland creatures from some very dangerous animals."

I gulped and wondered just how dangerous the animals round here could get. "I... well that is... I just thought that maybe, perhaps, well that I could visit him."

"Prison visitors need a permit." Badger relaxed a little. "The prison is in the middle of the wood and Hedgehog is allowed one visit each week. He has to request a permit from me. He's never asked for one yet, so I don't suppose he's going to want a strange puppy visiting."

"I'm not that strange, am I?"

PC Badger shook his head.

I was a little crestfallen, but thanked PC Badger and carried on through the wood. Perhaps I could write to Hedgehog anyway, there was nothing to lose. I picked up a large stick and started dragging it home, stopping to chew it every time it felt a bit too heavy, until by the time I got home, there was only half a stick left. Squirrel was waiting on the bird table.

"I thought you weren't coming," she said, flitting her beautiful red tail from side to side, as she climbed down the base of the table.

"Sorry, I was trying to drag this stick back for building the den. Bringing one stick at a time is going to be a very slow process and it really doesn't help that I forgot what it was for and stopped to chew it. I do find sticks so hard to resist. Building a den is going to be hard work. I think I may need to find some help. Are there any builders in the forest? Not that the pocket money I get from the Boss would stretch to paying them."

"I'm sure we'll find a way somehow, Alfie. You're always good at things like that." Squirrel was busy gathering up the crumbs underneath the bird table.

I felt myself blushing. "You don't think the project is too ambitious?"

"Well it will be very difficult, but I'm sure we'll get there in the end."

Then we sat in the sunshine, thinking our separate thoughts. I was thinking of ways to make the den bigger and I imagined that Squirrel was thinking of ways to make it cosier. In all the excitement, I almost forgot I was supposed to be writing to Hedgehog.

It was early afternoon before I sat down with a piece of paper and began to write.

House at the end of the Bridleway
Edge of the Wood

The Woodland Prison
The Darkest bit of the Wood
Somewhere near the Middle
The Wood at the Bottom of the Garden

March 14th

Dear Mr Hedgehog,

My name is Alfie. I'm a four-month-old puppy living just on the edge of the wood. I heard all the helicopters looking for you the other day and was very sorry to hear that you had to go back to the prison. It can't be very much fun for you being there. I wondered whether I could come to visit you.

Yours sincerely,
Alfie Dog

Then I folded the letter, put it in the envelope and went off to find one of the magpies who run the Woodland Postal Service. From what I'd been told the magpies were reasonably good, but had a tendency to rifle through the envelopes in search of any brightly coloured bits for their nests. It was possible to pay extra to get a carrion crow escort, but I didn't have enough left from my pocket money, so I hoped that it would get there. Then I just needed to wait for a reply.

A couple of days later I was up much earlier than usual,

waiting for the post. I had no idea how long it took for letters to be delivered, or even whether I would get any reply from Hedgehog. I thought about it very carefully and decided I should tell Squirrel what I was doing.

Once breakfast was out of the way, I rushed into the woods and down the bridleway to Squirrel's house. She was just waking up from a cold few days when I knocked. Even once she'd answered the door, it took a little bit of time for her to come round. She rubbed the sleep out of her eyes with her paws and yawned a dainty, feminine yawn.

I put the kettle on and waited quietly until she was washed and awake. As she took her acorn shell cup of coffee she said, "What day is it, Alfie?"

"Thursday."

"Oh dear, we really mustn't lose any more time before getting started on the plans for the den."

I kicked my paws nervously. "No, of course, but before we do, there's something I need to tell you." I swallowed hard.

Squirrel sank down into the settee next to me. "Yes?"

I didn't know what to say but managed, "It's Hedgehog."

"Oh no," Squirrel jumped up and spilt her coffee. "Has he escaped again?"

I was concentrating so hard on what I was going to say that I became very confused. "Why? Have you heard something?"

"No, you were about to tell me something. I thought maybe that was what you were going to say."

"Aah, no. I've written to him."

Squirrel gasped. "What? Oh Alfie, why ever would you want to do that?" She sat down again, with her paws to her head, looking very worried.

"I thought it might be nice to see him. I thought he might be lonely. Anyway, I sent a letter, but I haven't had a reply."

"I see." She raised her eyebrows. "Well I do hope you know what you're doing." She shook her head. "It can take at least a couple of days for a letter to be delivered. I'd really rather you weren't doing that, Alfie. Oh well." She gave a little sigh. "While you're waiting, let's see if we can start drawing out what the den is going to look like." I knew she was trying to cheer me up and I felt grateful.

We spent the rest of the morning drawing the den, until by lunchtime we had drawn fifteen different pictures and were quite convinced it wasn't going to look like any of them.

As it turned out, I didn't have very long to wait for a reply from Hedgehog because the following morning the magpies flew by and dropped one letter, on which was scrawled

'Alfie Dog
House at the end of the Bridleway
Edge of the Wood'.

I rushed inside to find a quiet corner. My heart pounded as I carefully tore the corner. I was so eager to see what Hedgehog had written. Once I opened the envelope a small card fell out, which said simply 'Woodland Prison – Visitor permit. Valid on Saturday 18th March'. I gasped. There was also a single sheet of paper, which in a very rough hand said,

'Dear Alfie

I really have no idea why you want to visit me. I haven't had any visitors since I was brought here ten months ago. But if you insist on coming, then you'd best come Saturday before I change my mind.

Hedgehog'

That was settled. Tomorrow I would see Hedgehog. All that remained was to tell Squirrel and to get some directions to the prison. When I went back outside, one of the magpies was on the bird table and presuming he must know the way from deliveries and collections I called over to him.

"Excuse me, but can you tell me the route to the Woodland Prison, please?"

The magpie muttered to himself as he finished the seed he was eating. "What do you want with a visiting permit for the prison? Magpies make little enough to live on as it is, the only way we keep going are the extra bits we pick up from the letters. Then you have us running errands to and from the prison. We spend most of our time trying to keep out of that place. We have to dodge PC Badger every time we go there in case he wants us to 'assist with his enquiries'."

"I'm sorry. I thought it was your job to deliver the post?"

"That doesn't mean we have to enjoy it. Everyone has to earn a crust or two."

"Would you mind telling me which direction I have to go in, to get to the prison?"

"Well I fly in a straight line, so it isn't too difficult for me." He hopped to the ground. "For you though, if you turn right about half way along the bridleway, just keep going until the trees get much closer together, then turn right again, head along the path into the undergrowth and if you stay on the path for as far as you can get through the plants, you can't miss it."

"Thanks." I started to wonder if I had the courage to go. It had been bad enough in the nearer part of the wood with Rabbit. I wondered what animals might live in the darkest part of the woods.

I headed off into the wood and met Squirrel coming the other way. "Do you think there are any tigers?"

"Tigers? Whatever are you talking about? I was just coming to tell you that I'm off to meet up with my brothers and see if they're all right after the winter."

"Sorry. I was just thinking about what sort of animals live in the darkest part of the wood and I wondered if there were any tigers. I'm going to see Hedgehog tomorrow and to be honest, I think I'm scared."

"Oh dear, oh no." She put down her basket. "You received a letter then?"

"Yes and a visitor's permit for tomorrow. A magpie told me how to find the prison and now I'm worrying about what I might meet on the way. You travel around the woods quite a lot, Squirrel; do you think I need to be scared?"

"Alfie, there aren't any tigers around here. I think there are wild boars somewhere about, but I don't think they come as far as our wood. Do you mind spiders and insects?"

I smiled. "I have to deal with spiders for the Boss, they aren't a problem. Are wild boars friendly? If I see one should I introduce myself?"

"I don't think so, but then I don't think you will meet any. Now I really must be off. Please be careful seeing

Hedgehog."

"Yes, thank you. Good luck finding your brothers. I hope they're all right." I waved a paw after her as she ran back up the nearest tree. I wished she was coming with me to the prison, even if she didn't want to see Hedgehog. I felt so much braver when Squirrel was nearby.

CHAPTER 5
THE WOODLAND PRISON

I set off for the prison early on Saturday morning. I wasn't sure whether I was more worried about my journey or what I'd say to Hedgehog. I followed the route that Magpie described, sniffing the air for tigers as I went.

Very soon, the trees grew closer and closer together and the path became narrower and narrower. There were plants closing in on the path and the wood became darker. I felt very small and very frightened, even without the scent of wild boar. I wasn't sure I'd remembered the directions correctly and was worried I was going to be lost forever. I wondered if perhaps I should turn around. It would feel much less scary with someone else's paw to hold. Although if the someone else were to scream...

I could hear a rustling in the undergrowth. I stopped. The hairs on the back of my neck were standing up and I pricked my ears to listen. There was another rustle. I tried to breathe as quietly as I could, but I could hear my heart pounding.

Rabbit leaped out from behind a bush and, in my surprise, I fell over altogether.

"Ha ha, thought I'd make you jump."

"Oh, Rabbit! I thought it was a tiger."

"Sorry to disappoint you, old chap. I could try roaring for you."

"No, please don't. You gave me such a fright."

"That's good then. I haven't lost the knack. What are

you up to?"

I wasn't sure I wanted to tell Rabbit I was visiting Hedgehog, but I couldn't see what else I could say. "I was just going for a walk."

"Really? Funny sort of just going for a walk. Besides you've dropped this." He picked up my visitor permit and passed it to me. He was grinning.

"Thanks." I said. "I suppose you could come with me, if you'd like to."

"Me, set foot in the prison through the front door? No fear. I might try scaling the wall one day though. Although there's always the risk they might keep me. Then I'd have to break out. Why don't I meet you later?" And without making any arrangement, he bounced back into the trees.

I carried on along the path feeling rather brighter, despite the fright he'd given me. I heard a crackle of twigs. "You can't catch me twice, Rabbit."

"Rabbit? I'm no rabbit. Now who goes there?"

I took a step forward and realised that the bushes made way for a clearing. This time there was a very serious looking weasel blocking my path.

"Al... Hhhuu." I coughed. "Alfie Dog. I'm looking for the Woodland Prison."

"Well you've found it. Now what do you want?"

I gulped and stepped backwards. "I er, I, well I." I started to unfold my visitor permit.

"Don't move again until I say so," said the weasel.

"Oh dear! I'm sorry. I just came to visit Hedgehog. I was trying to get my Visitor Permit to show you."

The weasel stood back a pace. "Pass the permit to me."

I got the permit and presented it to the weasel. I don't know if he could read it with my paw shaking so much.

"Straight on to the main entrance and sign in at the

desk." He nodded toward the building.

"Thank you." I wished more than anything that I'd stayed at home. I was being treated like a criminal even though I was only a visitor and with the exception of the acorns, I wasn't aware I'd done anything very wrong.

The prison was built out of the local stones packed together with earth and had a menacing look, probably because of the absence of any greenery climbing up the walls. From the main entrance, another weasel led me along a corridor to a little room with a few tables. At each turn, the door ahead was unlocked until we went through and then relocked behind me with a clanging thud as the key turned. I was feeling very uncomfortable and began to worry that I wasn't going to be allowed out ever again. What was I doing here? I'd never met Hedgehog and I'd absolutely no idea what to say to him. I reminded myself that no matter what he'd done wrong, everyone deserved to have a friend. I just wasn't sure why I'd decided that friend should be me!

A thin hedgehog, with small round glasses perched on his little brown nose was ushered into the visiting room by another guard. He was just like any other hedgehog. I think I was disappointed that he didn't look at all scary. I'd imagined him with tattoos on all his visible flesh and maybe a body piercing or two. His nose twitched slightly and he had a broad smile as he came towards me.

"Hello, er, er."

"Hello, young Alfie." Hedgehog sat opposite to me. "How good of you to come all this way to see me. I haven't had any visitors since I was brought here last year."

In my relief that Hedgehog was friendly, all of a sudden I began to talk. "I heard about you when the helicopter was out searching for you. Squirrel says you've done something called money laundering and identity theft, but I don't think it's very nice of them to lock you up for leaving your money in your pocket and going out in fancy dress. I don't know whether you know Squirrel. She's really beautiful. She has lovely ginger hair and I feel myself going red every time I see her. She's gone to see her brothers. I'm living in the house at the end of the bridleway. But then you know that because you wrote to me…"

"Oh, Alfie do pause for breath. You're making me feel quite tired." His spines moved in waves as he spoke.

I must have been talking for quite some time. I opened my mouth to carry on but Weasel called that visiting time was over. "Oh but, Hedgehog you haven't told me about you."

Hedgehog laughed. "No, young Alfie I think we may have run out of time. It's been lovely to see you. Do you think you might like to see me again?"

Before I knew what I was saying, I said, "Oh yes please. I would love that."

I had a very heavy feeling watching the guards come to take Hedgehog back to his cell. It had felt bad enough just coming in as a visitor, it must have been awful for Hedgehog to have to stay there for so long.

After Hedgehog was led away, a weasel came to escort me back to the main entrance. As I walked back through the forest, it was so good to feel the breeze and the freedom of being outside. I had absolutely no idea why I'd said I'd go back and visit Hedgehog again.

I was right. Hedgehog was much too nice to be in prison. I really didn't understand why they thought he was bad. The prison was quite awful, but I thought it would help Hedgehog if I did go back. I was deep in my own thinking, pushing my way through the undergrowth. It was a very dark part of the wood and it was impossible to see where I was going. I used my front paws to feel the way forwards and then shuffled my back paws to meet them. I was moving my front paws forwards again when I suddenly found myself sliding down a bank into a ditch that was completely overgrown with plants. It was a deep ditch and the sides seemed to rush past me. I yelped in pain as my ankle twisted. After what seemed like forever, I landed with a thud in the squelchy thick black mud at the bottom of the ditch.

"Help!" I could be stuck here forever. "Help!" I couldn't move and could see no way I was going to get out. "Help!" I was too far from the prison guards for them to hear me and a long way from the main track. "Help!" I knew the Boss would miss me when I didn't come home for tea, but that was ages away and even if she missed me, she had no idea where I was going. "Help!" Squirrel knew, but she would be away for a couple of days and even then it might be several days before she realised I wasn't around. "Help!" What if the wild boar found me now, or a tiger. I could starve down here, which was probably even worse. "Help!" I had no idea what to do next. It would only be if they heard me that anyone would... "Help!"

I tried to stand up and put weight on my ankle, but it was hurting, so I sat down and looked around at the ditch. There were steep sides all around me and I couldn't see any way that I was going to get out on my own. I hobbled to the other side to see if it was as bad as it looked. "Help!" I was trying to work out if the undergrowth was strong enough to pull myself up, but as I tugged at some ivy it broke off in my paw. I was starting to feel very worried and very small. "Help!"

"Is that you, Alfie?"

"Oh, Rabbit thank goodness. I'm stuck at the bottom of this ditch and I can't get out."

"You can't catch me that easily, Alfie."

"No, Rabbit really, it's true. I need help. I think I've hurt my ankle."

Rabbit paused. "Really?"

"Yes, really. Rabbit, please, this isn't a game. Can you get help?"

"You can depend on Rabbit old chap. Just you wait there," and I heard him trying to bounce through the undergrowth.

I sat in the mud feeling miserable, wishing I'd never tried to visit the prison and wishing more than anything that Squirrel was there. I hadn't been waiting long when I heard animals above.

"Now don't you worry, young Dog."

I had never been so grateful to hear PC Badger's voice.

"We're going to climb down and get you out of there in no time. Weasel, hold the ladder for me. Rabbit, you stand there and don't let go of that rope." Then first a paw and then a trousered leg appeared as PC Badger very carefully climbed down a rope ladder into the ditch to where I was.

"Now can you put any weight on your leg, Alfie?"

I tried to stand and winced.

"Ok, sit down a minute." Then deftly PC Badger bandaged my ankle. "Now lean on me." He helped me up. "I'll go up the ladder first then if you hang onto the rope, we'll pull you up." He disappeared and then I heard him saying, "Now altogether, Weasel, Rabbit, pull. That's it, gently. Now, pull." And I was gradually pulled up the side of the ditch until I was back on safe ground.

"I think that's enough excitement for one day. We need to get you home to get some rest. Lean on me as you go."

Then badger supported me as I hobbled the rest of the way out through the undergrowth.

"Thanks, Rabbit," I said to my anxious friend.

"Don't mention it. I'm always looking for an odd bit of excitement. It's unusual to find some without getting into trouble."

It was two days later when Squirrel appeared. She was waiting on the bird table when I went outside and immediately hopped down and ran to give me a hug.

"I'm so glad you're ok. I heard all about your accident and I was so worried about you. I shall never say another bad thing about Rabbit. If it hadn't been for him… Oh, I just can't bear to think."

"I'm glad you're back, Squirrel. I missed you." I could feel a wide smile creeping right across my face.

"I missed you too, Alfie. Now why don't you tell me how you got on at the prison?"

"It was scary. I don't really want to go through the wood on my own again, but I've promised to go back. It's so sad seeing him locked up. I feel sorry for him. What I can't understand is why someone should be put in prison for washing their money."

"Oh, Alfie." Squirrel laughed so much that tears started to stream down her face. "That isn't what he did. Money laundering isn't about washing your money in the way you wash your clothes. He stole lots of money."

"Well of course I knew that really," I said, trying to cover my embarrassment. "Actually, I didn't know that at all."

"Sit down and I'll tell you about it."

We sat on the grass and she began. "Hedgehog has been involved in some very bad things. He started by stealing and then gradually worked his way up in the crime world.

In the end, he became an expert in forgery and then computer fraud. Forgery is where you make copies of things, where the original is valuable and then pretend that your copy is real. Computer fraud is using your computer to access other computers, pretending to be them and stealing from them. ID theft is where you 'borrow' someone else's identity so you can take something of value or go somewhere you wouldn't otherwise be able to go. And money laundering is where you take money that has come from something bad, like selling drugs or stealing and then you make it so it can't be followed back to the original crime. That way you can use the money without being caught for the crime it came from."

"And you're saying that Hedgehog has done all those things, the very same Hedgehog that I went to see yesterday?"

"Yes." she nodded. "When Hedgehog was arrested, he was found to have opened bank accounts all over the world in lots of different names and moved money that had been stolen from the Woodland Bank to a numbered account in Switzerland."

"So he didn't dress up as a computer or wash his coins? I do wish you'd told me all that before I went to see him yesterday."

"I thought you already knew."

"I suppose Hedgehog must think I'm stupid. I've said I'll see him again, whatever am I going to do? I did rather enjoy talking to him." What I didn't say to Squirrel was that I was more than a little bit interested by what she'd just told me and I wanted to ask Hedgehog if it was true. "I've given him my word and none of that changes how dreadful it must be to be locked up. Maybe he's not like that anymore. Maybe he's a different Hedgehog now."

"I think being a different Hedgehog was what got him into trouble in the first place." Squirrel sighed. "You know, Alfie, you really are a very dear puppy."

CHAPTER 6
HEDGEHOG'S LIFE STORY

With only five weeks to go before the planning meeting, we needed to get to work on the den.

"Who can we use as the builders?" I asked.

"Well, there are two companies that I know of in the woods, 'Beaver Builders' and 'Mole Construction'." Squirrel walked across the page to draw the line for the roof of the den. "I sometimes wish my legs were as long as yours. I just can't stretch far enough. Do you really think it needs to be as big as this?" Squirrel stood on my shoulders to get a better view.

"I don't really know." I sighed flopping down. I'd forgotten Squirrel was on my back. She only just managed to cling on in time. "I just seem to keep growing."

"You have grown at quite an alarming rate. I wanted to talk to you about that. The thing is..." She paused and wrung her hands. "I wonder if you'd mind sitting somewhere other than my settee. I'm not sure that it's really grown with you." Then quickly she added, "I do like the fireplace you want."

We carried on working on the drawings, with me changing my mind almost every time Squirrel had finished a few lines and the pile of paper that we put aside, as 'out of date' drawings, grew bigger and bigger.

"Hang on, you've asked for that before." Squirrel started searching through the pile of drawings. "Oh, but the doorway was different. Tell me again, how do you want the sitting room?"

"Well, I thought it might be slightly rounded."

"You mean like this?" Squirrel searched through the pile again and presented me with another drawing.

"What I really meant was with enough room for my basket just here." I pointed to the corner.

"Like this?" said Squirrel, pulling yet another picture out of the pile.

"Perhaps more like that first one you showed me."

"Oh, Alfie, I've had enough for now. We'll get a new sheet of paper out later and then we can start again."

There was a rustling.

"Was that you, Squirrel?"

"I thought it came from outside."

I looked out and a Magpie spat a letter in my general direction.

I turned the letter over in my paws. "Oh, Squirrel! It's got the Woodland Prison logo on the back." I tore it open and took out the card, it read, 'Woodland Prison – Visitor Permit Saturday 25thMarch'.

"Squirrel, look, it's from Hedgehog. Whatever am I going to do?" I stepped on the corner of the latest plans, leaving a muddy paw print. "Oh why did I say I would see him again? I don't want to go through the woods on my own. Oh, Squirrel do you think you could come with me, so it doesn't seem so scary?"

"Oh, Alfie, I'm sorry. I've arranged to go back to see my brothers again this Saturday. I'm sure Hedgehog would understand if you wrote to him and said you couldn't go."

"But that wouldn't be true. It isn't that I can't go, it's that I'm scared. Poor Hedgehog, he might have done lots of bad things, but I am the only visitor he's had in a whole year, it's no wonder he's hoping I'll go back." I paced up and down as I spoke. "I've made up my mind. I'm not going to let him down. I gave him my word."

"Alfie, I'm so proud of you."

I had to turn away to hide my embarrassment. "Thank you."

We went back to drawing the den in silence and this time I didn't change my mind and it wasn't long before we'd got a rough picture of a den that we both thought looked rather good.

Saturday morning arrived and I was even more eager than usual to get breakfast out of the way. I was as ready as I could be, to walk to the darkest part of the woods. It's always best to set off on a full stomach, just in case I get a little bit lost.

It was brighter than the previous week and although the canopy of trees crowded in from all sides, a little more light was sneaking through the branches. I felt more confident of the direction I was going in and the journey passed much more quickly than before.

After the initial shout of "Halt, who goes there," from Weasel, the way was cleared as soon as I replied. The greeting wasn't warm, but I was happy to settle for it being rather less threatening. Once I'd gone through all the signing in and being taken into the visitor's room, Hedgehog was brought through to see me. He seemed cheerful and after an enthusiastic, "Hello, young Alfie Dog, I'm so glad you came." I started to feel quite glad I was there too.

"You must have thought I was a very silly dog, when I didn't know what money laundering was. Squirrel has told me all about it."

"I thought she would." As he smiled his nose wrinkled and then he rubbed his chin. "Last week you told me all about Alfie Dog, this week I'd like to tell you all about Hedgehog. When I've finished you can decide for yourself whether you want to see me again. I did wonder whether you'd come this week and I'm touched that you have."

"I gave you my word. My mum always told me that if I gave someone my word, I should always keep it."

There was a long pause whilst Hedgehog seemed lost in some distant thoughts then he began. "I was born in a wood a little way from here. The trees were much the same and life carried on, as it does outside this very prison. Then as so often happens, when I was very young, my dad left, and my mum tried as hard as she could to bring me up on her own. When I was still quite small I was left alone in the world, orphaned. I was probably about eight months old when that happened. I was one of the lucky ones. A couple of hedgehogs quite near here adopted me. They didn't have any hoglets of their own. They were much older, probably six or seven years old at the time. They gave me a good home and a lot of love and I shall always be grateful, but they both died while I was a teenager and I decided after everything I'd been through I'd just have to make it on my own.

Well one thing led to another and before I knew it, I'd fallen in with a bad set of friends and was stealing small items to get money for food. I was in the Wayward Hedgehog Centre on and off and met up with some more experienced criminals, who taught me a thing or two. After my first spell in the Woodland Prison, I decided that I was living a mug's game and planned one final crime before moving on to start a new life. The robbery was all part of a bigger operation, with a number of the other criminals who I'd met in here the first time. I can't say I'm proud of it, but robbing the Woodland Bank went to plan. I wasn't actually the one doing the robbery, but I produced a couple of fraudulent identities and accessed their computers to give security clearance to the ones who were doing the robbery. Then I dealt with investing and laundering the money. PC Badger turned up to arrest me when I was packing my few meagre possessions into a little knotted handkerchief. I was about to set off for a new life in the sun."

Hedgehog paused, but I didn't feel I should fill the silence, so I waited.

"Alfie, one thing I've realised in here is that you can try to run away from your troubles, but you can never run away from yourself. Money isn't going to make me happy. It will never be a substitute for the family I haven't got. When they let me out of here in May, I'm going to stay in the forest and try to put right some of the harm I've done over the years."

I didn't know what to say. I hadn't met my dad, but I'd been lucky, being adopted by the Boss. I was happy. Perhaps I didn't actually want to live in the den. "Hedgehog, if I manage to build the den, would you like to live in it when you're released?"

A tear formed in the corner of his eye and in a choked voice he said, "That's the kindest thing anyone has said or done for me in four years. Alfie, I would be honoured." And he clasped both of his tiny paws around mine and just sat there as the tears flowed.

Once Hedgehog wiped his eyes, we spent the rest of the visit planning the alterations to the den. They now needed to include 'Hedgehog's wing' with a little bedroom and sitting room of his own.

On my way home, I began to wonder whether Squirrel was going to understand what I'd done and I thought about how best to break the news to her. "You see, Squirrel."

"Well it's like this, Squirrel." It was no good there just didn't seem to be any right way of doing it. It might help to get Squirrel to visit Hedgehog the following week. If she got to know what he was really like, then maybe she would think it was a good idea.

I was deep in thought when Rabbit bounced out carrying a ladder. "Just the person?"

"Hello, Rabbit."

"I thought we could mount a rescue mission," Rabbit said putting the ladder on the ground.

"Oh no! Is someone else trapped?"

"Good heavens no. I thought you wanted to get Hedgehog out of prison." Rabbit scratched behind his ear.

"Well yes and no. We have to wait until he comes out. It won't be long."

"Oh why wait until then. I reckon if we can get this ladder up to the wall, I could jump down the other side and we'd be inside in no time."

"I don't think we're supposed to do that."

"Never mind if we're supposed to do it. Let's have some fun. I'll do it on my own if you're not coming." Then he picked up the ladder and carried on into the wood.

I hesitated. Of course, I did want Hedgehog out, but after the trouble I'd got into over the acorns I decided not to follow him.

After everything Hedgehog said, I wanted to give the Boss a hug and tell her how much I loved living with her. Perhaps now was the time to let on that I could say a little more than woof.

When I went through the door, I didn't have chance to say anything before the Boss lifted me up and gave me a big hug. I melted into her arms and nudged her hand towards tickling my tummy. I nuzzled up. "I just wanted to say thank you for giving me a home. I do like living here." Then she gave me another hug. She didn't seem the least bit surprised that I was talking to her.

I was on the way to see Squirrel the next morning when I saw Rabbit. "Rabbit, how did it go yesterday?"

"It didn't exactly. It would have done, but PC Badger had a word with me and we decided it wasn't a good idea. I might try again later if you want to come."

"I don't think I will. Thank you."

"Well please yourself." And he bounced off.

I didn't think I'd mention Rabbit's antics to Squirrel. Somehow I didn't think she'd understand. It was going to be difficult enough getting her to understand about including Hedgehog in the den.

CHAPTER 7
SQUIRREL GOES TO VISIT
HEDGEHOG

When I arrived at Squirrel's house she was sweeping the leaves away outside the front door.

"Hello."

"Oh, there you are, Alfie," she said as though I was late for something. "I thought you could give me a hand. There's so very much to do. Could you get some water from the stream to wash the windows and then help me bring in some of the acorns from the store? Then when we've done that I need to make up the beds and dust in the spare bedroom." She handed me the bucket and I knew better than to ask any questions until she was more in control.

By the time we'd finished and sat down for a cup of tea, I felt it was safe to talk. "Squirrel, who exactly is coming to stay?"

"Oh, Alfie, I'm sorry. I've been so anxious and nervous I hadn't realised you didn't know. When I went to see my brothers last week, I met one of their friends and well, I don't know quite how to put this, but I rather liked him. Then when I saw my brothers yesterday, he was there again and he and my younger brother said they'd like to come over to our side of the wood to see me and find out more about where I live. So they're coming tomorrow and staying overnight."

My heart sank. My Squirrel, or at least that was how I saw her. I knew I was a dog and not a squirrel, but Squirrel was lovely and she was my friend. I didn't imagine she might find a boy squirrel that she liked. I tried to sound pleased for her. "That's great."

I twiddled the disc on my collar. "I went to see Hedgehog yesterday."

Squirrel clapped her hands together. "I had quite forgotten in all the excitement. How is he?"

"Well he's fine, but I was wondering whether you would come with me to visit him next week."

"Who me? Well I'm really not sure." Her eyes suddenly looked very large and she seemed quite horrified by the prospect.

"I would really like you to and besides, I've sort of asked him if he'd like to live in my den when he comes out of prison." She went completely quiet. "I'm sorry, Squirrel I know I shouldn't have asked him without talking to you first. It was just that he told me his life story and it was so sad and I felt such a privileged puppy that I wanted to do something nice for him. I didn't want to upset you. You are the dearest friend any dog could have. I'll go on my own next week and tell him I was wrong to ask him."

"No, Alfie, you can't do that. You are such a big-hearted dog, that's one of the reasons I like you so much. Why don't you tell me Hedgehog's life story and see what I think?"

I told Squirrel the story, exactly as Hedgehog had told me and when I finished Squirrel dried her eyes on the corner of her handkerchief and wrapped her arms around my front paw. "Of course he can live in the den and I will come with you to see him next week."

I gave her a little squeeze. "Thank you. I've got to go now. I hope you have a nice time with your brother and his friend." I was surprised to find I meant it. Perhaps it was knowing that whatever happened, I wasn't going to lose her friendship.

When I next went to see Squirrel, I was looking forward to hearing how she had got on with her visitors.

"My brother came on his own," she said kicking a leaf.

I brightened up immediately.

"His friend met another girl squirrel last weekend and decided not to come."

Suddenly the sun was shining and a whole choir of birds were singing in harmony.

"I spent some time starting to fill in our planning application form too," she continued. "I thought we could take it with us tomorrow to get Hedgehog to help us with the difficult bits."

"That's a great idea." I felt relieved that she was still coming to see Hedgehog. Suddenly it felt as though it had been a perfect week.

We arranged to meet the following morning, outside Squirrel's house, as this was on the way to the prison. When I arrived, Squirrel was looking very nervous and fiddling with the corner of the folder containing the planning application.

"Do I need to bring anything else?" she asked then added, "Do you think this is all going to be all right?"

"Of course it will… You look quite lovely."

Squirrel blushed. "Shall we go?"

When we arrived at the prison, the weasels were much more polite to Squirrel than they had been to me in previous weeks. In fact, nothing was too much trouble. I glared at them. Then when we got into the visiting room, Hedgehog had put on his best clothes, well the best they let him have in prison and had combed his hair very carefully. Anyone would have thought he was having a visit from royalty. The prison probably didn't get many pretty female visitors. It's funny how such a beautiful animal as Squirrel, has never shown the slightest vanity and despite all this fuss, simply carried on as normal.

I introduced Squirrel to Hedgehog and she suddenly seemed very shy.

"I don't suppose you've seen Rabbit have you?" I asked Hedgehog.

"Good heavens, has he finally been caught for some of his escapades?" Hedgehog asked shaking his head.

"Well not that I know of. It was just that he was going to rescue you."

Hedgehog rocked with laughter. "Oh dear," he said wiping away a tear. "Don't tell me he was coming in here of his own accord. They'd never let him out again. The best thing you can do, young Alfie is not get involved with any of his schemes."

I wriggled slightly on my chair. "Oh, he's not so bad and he was the one who rescued me the other week."

"Be that as it may. He's not so good either. Now I'm going to ask Squirrel here to keep an eye on you." He winked at Squirrel. "I don't want to hear you've been getting involved with Rabbit."

"Right." I then quickly changed the subject. We spent the rest of the visit trying to finish the plans for the den, as we needed to submit the application within the week, to be in time for the Woodland Council meeting.

Squirrel had already filled in most of the forms, but there were some sections she was unsure about. "I thought you might know more about things like that than we did," she said to Hedgehog.

Hedgehog took the form and looked at it closely, then he picked up Squirrel's pen and started to write.

We then worked out how much the fee would be to

submit the plans.

"I'll write a cheque," said Hedgehog.

"I can pay you back." I counted on my paws. "I've got just enough in my savings account."

"Nonsense, young Alfie, it's the least I can do after you've been so good as to include me in the project."

I wondered which bank Hedgehog used, but thought it better not to ask. I supposed it was unlikely that after stealing their money the Woodland Bank would want him to have an account with them.

By the time we had to leave the Woodland Prison, it was as though we were all old friends.

"I don't know why I was so worried," said Squirrel as we walked away.

Then from nowhere Rabbit bounced out. "G'day folks."

"Hello, Rabbit. What are you up to?" I was always pleased to see him.

"Hello, Rabbit. Come along, Alfie." Squirrel took my paw firmly.

"I was looking for an adventure. Do you want to come?"

"No, thank you." Squirrel started to walk away.

"I've got nothing on," I said, turning back. "I think I might go with Rabbit for a while."

"Alfie! You know what Hedgehog said."

"Oh yes?" Rabbit tipped his head on one side. "What did Hedgehog say?"

"Oh, nothing important." I waved a paw. "See you later, Squirrel." I couldn't help thinking she looked sad as she walked away.

"Come on then." Rabbit bounced on ahead of me, heading towards the far side of the wood. "Hey, look there."

I looked across at a fallen tree, the roots freshly out of

the soil.

"We could build your den with bits of that tree. Come on."

"But Rabbit, what about needing permission?" I panted as I caught up.

"Rabbits don't need permission for things." And with that he set about breaking some of the twigs off the tree.

I wasn't sure I wanted my den just there, but Rabbit's enthusiasm was catching and I soon found myself doing whatever he said.

"If you put this branch up as the middle, it's got a good 'Y' shaped bit, yes that's right. Now lean the other sticks up against it."

I was concentrating hard on what he was telling me and I didn't hear PC Badger coming up behind.

"Hu Hum."

I froze.

"What's going on here, young Alfie?" He gave me a serious look.

"It was just Rabbit." I turned to where Rabbit had been standing to find that he had vanished. "Sorry, sir. We were just…"

"Well don't, young Dog. I don't want to see you getting into any more trouble. I thought it was a bad idea you going to see that Hedgehog."

"Oh no, sir, it wasn't anything to do with Hedgehog. He told me not to spend time with Rabbit."

"Well on this occasion, he's probably right. Now run along, before I take you down to the station."

I wandered off with my tail between my legs, wondering how it was that Rabbit never managed to be caught. I realised I'd have to go back to doing the den the right way instead.

Over the next few days, Squirrel and I set about putting the finishing touches to the plans to submit with the application.

"If we build the den around an oak tree, we could build a funnel into the roof to catch the acorns and bring them straight down into our storage area," I said as Squirrel tried to keep a line straight.

She chewed the end of her pencil. "It sounds very exciting, but if it were that easy, wouldn't someone have done it before? Wouldn't it bring all the water in too?"

"Oh bother. No, hang on a minute. If we include a basket shaped grate, underneath, all the water will drain away and leave you with just the acorns."

"It's a lovely idea. It would save me an awful lot of work each year."

I suddenly jumped up and down. "I've worked it out. If we make the den a bit bigger we could build it round a chestnut tree too. Then we could build another funnel with a separate pipe in the middle for the chimney. Then by the time the chestnuts come out of the chute at the bottom they will already be roasted. I think chestnuts might be safe for dogs. After all, humans can eat them."

"Aren't they the wrong type for roasting? Wouldn't it be more fun to sit side by side around the fire, roasting chestnuts?"

Although I felt a little disappointed, the thought of a cosy winter's evening, sitting close to Squirrel, roasting chestnuts, did sound rather lovely.

Hedgehog's little suite of rooms was off to one side, to give him some privacy and on the other side of the den was a special area for me to sit and work on my computer. There was room for sitting by the fireside and room for sitting in a chair and reading and of course room for a bed to curl up in. I wagged my tail with excitement and accidentally knocked the papers onto the floor. Squirrel was so happy thinking about the acorn catcher that she didn't even get cross with me and we spent an enjoyable ten minutes picking them all up and putting them back in order.

CHAPTER 8
ALFIE DOG PRIVATE
INVESTIGATOR

I paw-delivered the planning application to the Woodland Council pigeon-hole. I wasn't sure whether it was just called a 'pigeon-hole' or whether there might be a pigeon somewhere who didn't appreciate having letters stuck in his doorway. As soon as I posted it, I began to worry whether I had included everything, but it was too late to check. We had submitted the application a whole day before the deadline and as I padded home, I felt very proud and very tired. All we could do now was wait.

When I got home, I fell into a deep sleep and dreamed I was in a court-room. PC Badger seemed to be the judge and was saying, "Alfie Dog you are charged with submitting a planning application for the building of a den in this forest. How do you plead?"

"I'm guilty, I'm guilty, I'm guilty," I shouted out and woke with a start to find the Boss next to me stroking my paw.

"I think you were having a nightmare. Is anything worrying you?"

I hadn't mentioned the den. I thought quickly. "It's about Hedgehog."

"What about Hedgehog?"

Having omitted the minor details that one of my best friends was a fraudster, a robber and a money launderer and was currently residing in prison, now didn't seem the right time to be completely honest. "It's just that he might have nowhere to live in a few weeks' time and I was wondering…"

"Hmm, you were wondering if he could come to live with us."

"How did you know that?"

"Just a hunch." She smiled. "Now why don't you get some sleep and we'll talk about it nearer the time, if he still hasn't got anywhere to live by then."

Knowing what a softie the Boss was, I rolled over for my tummy to be tickled and it wasn't long before I completely relaxed and fell into a deep and happy sleep.

When I next went to visit Hedgehog, I trudged through the undergrowth. Squirrel had gone for a picnic with her brothers. It was much more fun doing the journey when she was with me.

They would release Hedgehog from the prison quite soon. His escape attempt had only added two weeks to his sentence, but he'd been warned that any repeat would mean him having to stay another six months.

Without Squirrel the weasels were not nearly so nice and Hedgehog was in his usual scruffy prison outfit. A helicopter had flown over as I arrived at the prison gates and I was almost expecting the warders to turn me away at the entrance.

"You're here, Hedgehog," I said, when they led him through.

"Where else would I be?"

"Well with the helicopter, I thought you might have stepped outside again." I didn't like to say 'escaped' it sounded all wrong when you're actually inside the prison.

Hedgehog laughed. "Now what would be the point of that? When I ran away last time, I felt as though there was nothing out there for me and whether or not I was caught didn't really matter. I did it for the fun. It was a sudden opportunity and I took it. If I'd planned my escape better, I'd have taken my glasses and wouldn't have mistaken that broom for another Hedgehog. Now I've got a future and I don't want to spoil it. You and Squirrel have become like a family to me. I don't want to end up in here any longer than I have to."

Before I had chance to update Hedgehog on the planning application, he put his spectacles on his nose and continued. "Now, I think I need your help. I've had a letter this week that may not be all that it seems. What are you like at investigating?"

"You mean, like a detective? Looking for clues and trying to work something out?"

"That's exactly what I mean." He took the letter out of his pocket, unfolded it and smoothed it out carefully on the table. "This claims to come from a cousin who was a relative of my father. Now I didn't know my father and I was too young for my mother to have told me much about him that I'd remember. This cousin says he's been trying to trace me for some time. I'd like to feel excited that I have a relative, but it just seems a bit too convenient to turn up when I'm about to be released from prison. He may just be trying to get his paws on my money."

Suddenly I could see myself in the role of secret agent, unmasking the criminal intentions of another hedgehog. I came back to reality hearing Hedgehog saying, "So what do you think, Alfie? Will you do it?"

"But where would I start? I don't know how to investigate and I've got a bit big for hiding behind trees." He showed me the letter with a postmark that clearly said 'Magpie Post'. "Well I can tell it's been posted near here from the postmark. I'll give it a go, but I don't know if I'll find anything out." I folded the letter carefully and put it away for later.

"Good dog, that's the spirit."

Before we knew where the time had gone, it was time to leave and I watched sadly, as the guards led my friend away. I had thought it better not to mention my afternoon with Rabbit and PC Badger stopping me and giving me a warning.

Once I got away from the prison, I took the letter out and examined it carefully. It had a return address, but it was a nest-box number in a wood some way from here. How do you go about investigating the identity of a hedgehog? It's easy with dogs, I have both a tattoo and a microchip, but a hedgehog doesn't have any of those and because Hedgehog knows so little about his father, we don't even know of anyone we can ask. I began to wonder why I'd said I'd do it and thought that my best option was to wait until the following day and talk to Squirrel. Just then, Rabbit popped up, as he had an uncanny knack of doing.

"What are you up to, Alfie?"

I hesitated. Rabbit might be able to help me find the hedgehog, but I wasn't sure I should include him. "Nothing." I crossed my paw.

"You can't fool Rabbit that easily." He bounced over and grabbed the letter. "I see. What do we have here?" He scratched his ear with his back paw.

"Oh, Rabbit. Do give it back."

"Not until you tell me what it is."

"Ok, you can help me." I needed someone to help and there was no reason it shouldn't be rabbit. "If you give me the letter back I'll explain."

Rabbit passed me the letter and I spread it out in front of me. "Hedgehog wants to know whether he's got a cousin."

"Well that doesn't sound very exciting." Rabbit jumped up.

"Oh well it is," I said proudly. "He wants me to investigate to see if it's real."

We read the letter together.

"My dear long-lost cousin. I heard so much about you from my father, before he passed away. I have spent the last year trying to find you. I hope my letter finds you well. It would be wonderful to meet you after all this time.

Your loving cousin."

"Why's it so important?" Rabbit asked.

"Hedgehog isn't sure if it is a real cousin or just a hedgehog after his money." I explained.

Suddenly Rabbit understood. "Aah, and he wants you to find out."

"Exactly. There isn't much he can do from inside the prison, so he thought maybe I could try for him."

"What do we need then? A magnifying glass, a finger printing kit, maybe some invisible ink. I had a kit with all those in last Christmas."

I didn't like to tell Rabbit that I couldn't see us doing any fingerprinting. I agreed to meet him at the edge of the wood in half an hour.

Squirrel had joined me when Rabbit got back. I'd told her all about the letter, but had forgotten to mention that Rabbit was helping.

"Shh," said Squirrel as Rabbit approached.

He was peering through his magnifying glass as he walked. He held it up to Squirrel's eye as he got to us and she jumped backwards.

"Rabbit! You've told him already haven't you, Alfie. You don't need my help at all." She started to walk away.

"Oh, Squirrel, can't all three of us work together. This will be fun and we won't be getting into trouble."

"Rabbit always gets into trouble."

"Oh please, Squirrel." Rabbit dropped down on one knee and grinned up at her sweetly. "I promise I'll be good. I'll let you use my fingerprinting kit."

Squirrel gave a deep sigh. "All right, but if you misbehave…" I was in no doubt that I didn't want to get on the wrong side of Squirrel and I crossed my claws that Rabbit would keep his word.

"We could start by asking a few of the more trustworthy woodland animals whether they have relatives in the wood where the cousin says he lives." Squirrel was looking thoughtful.

"So not the magpies then." I laughed.

"Can't we start with the fingerprints on the letter?" Rabbit took the powder from his kit and beginning to dust the corner of the letter. "Look!" He held out the envelope as a fingerprint began to appear.

"But, Rabbit!" Squirrel sighed. "We've all touched the letter and besides we don't have any fingerprints to compare it with."

Rabbit's head dropped. "I just thought."

I was trying to think of things that would keep him interested. "Perhaps if we can find a contact in that wood, we may need to go over there to see them. It's a long way away though. I don't think we could get there very easily."

"Can we take their fingerprints?" Rabbit asked quietly.

"No, I don't think so." Squirrel shook her head.

"Not even a little bit?" Rabbit kicked the leaves with his paw.

"Rabbit!" Squirrel was beginning to sound annoyed.

"Ok, I can take a hint."

"Now all we need to do is find an animal with a relative we can talk to." I tried to bring everyone back to the problem.

"I think we should start with the deer. They seem to travel about quite a bit and have relatives in lots of places." Rabbit was frowning as though thinking was very hard work.

"You know, Rabbit," Squirrel said, that's the best idea you've had yet. "There's just one small problem."

"What's that?" I asked.

"Well, which of the law-abiding animals is going to want to help Hedgehog? He has stolen something from nearly all of them at one time or another. If we go up to any animal in this wood and say 'we're trying to help Hedgehog prevent an impostor from getting their hands on the money, which may or may not be the proceeds of crime, and may or may not have originally been taken from the Woodland Bank,' they aren't going to help. To be honest I think they'll walk away as soon as we say 'we're trying to help Hedgehog'." Squirrel sat down with her head in her paws.

"Do we have to tell them it's for Hedgehog?" Rabbit said.

"Well how else are we going to do it?" Squirrel didn't even look us as she spoke.

I had a sudden thought. "We could just say we're trying to find a hedgehog in the other wood without telling anyone why and just see if he exists. We can worry about whether he's really Hedgehog's cousin after we've found him."

"Alfie, that's one of your better ideas. I suppose if we

had to say any more, we could say we were trying to sort some help out for Hedgehog for when he comes out of prison. That might get a good response. Particularly if they think he might live a long way away from here." Squirrel sat smiling and seemed to have forgotten her earlier annoyance with Rabbit.

We set off into the wood to make some enquiries.

The ants were sure that the moles had mentioned having family in every wood, and the woodpecker said he sometimes flew over that way if that was any help. We were very careful not to mention Hedgehog and our plan seemed to be working out quite well.

"That's that then. We'll just have to go over there and then ask around when we get there. But how can we get there? We can't walk to the far wood. It's too far." I'd never walked nearly that far, not ever.

"And too dangerous," Squirrel said.

"Danger!" Rabbit's ears pricked up. "That sounds like fun."

"We could go by car." I expected them to tell me it was a silly idea.

"Can I drive?" Rabbit jumped up and down with excitement. "I've always wanted to drive. Oh let me."

"If he drives, I'm not coming." Squirrel glared at Rabbit.

"Will you two stop it? None of us would be driving. We don't know how. I thought we could get the Boss to take us. Well at least I thought I could get the Boss to take me. You two can stow away. It would be fun."

I thought Squirrel might refuse to stow away and was surprised when she clasped her little paws and said "A real stowaway, oh, Alfie how exciting. I never have any real adventures."

"Now all I need to do is get the Boss to take me to that

wood. You two make sure you are hiding in the hedge at the side of our garage tomorrow morning just before 10.00. Now here's the plan. What usually happens is that the Boss puts me in the car and fastens my seatbelt and then leaves the door open while she goes back to lock up. That's the point that you two get in and hide under the blanket on the seat."

"Ok, that's understood. At 09.50 hours, Squirrel and I will wait in the hedge ready to board the reconnaissance vehicle." Rabbit stood to attention and saluted.

"Rabbit, we're going in a car," Squirrel said impatiently.

"Yes, ma'am." Rabbit saluted Squirrel.

She looked at me and rolled her eyes.

"How do we get out of the car?" Squirrel asked.

"Good point. I'll create a diversion when we get there and you'll need to hop out without being seen. We'll do the same again to come back. Any more questions?" I looked at each of them in turn.

We wished each other luck and went our separate ways until the following morning.

CHAPTER 9
A VISIT TO THE DISTANT WOOD

I couldn't see the others as we went out to the car. Then as the Boss opened the door for me, I saw a tiny flag waving from the bottom of the bush and then being pulled back in. I waited until the Boss had gone back to lock the door and called, "Now!"

Squirrel and Rabbit ran out from the bush towards the car. It was only then that I realised Rabbit was wearing dark glasses and a hat and had binoculars on a string around his neck. He paused to give Squirrel a leg up into the car, put the binoculars to his eyes and looked around and then bounced himself up and in. I was just pulling the blanket over his ear when the Boss came back and shut the door.

The journey didn't take long and we were soon parking in the car park. I whispered down to the others, "Get ready." I was thinking hard about how I was going to divert attention from the car and as the Boss opened the door, I wagged my tail and shouted, "Look over there! That boy's got a big kite."

As she turned to look, Rabbit and Squirrel jumped down out of the car and scurried across to the nearest tree. We'd made it. Now all we needed to do was find Hedgehog's cousin.

As soon as I got some time to myself, I ran to find the other two. "Ok, let's go." We moved out of sight of the bench the Boss was sitting on reading a book. Then I took the letter out and looked at it. "Right, now we need to start asking around. Shall we go together or separately?"

"Together," chorused Squirrel and Rabbit, then looked at each other and laughed. It was good to see them getting on so well.

We started with some moles. They were in the middle of digging a new tunnel. Most moles seem to live on the edge of society and we decided they were more likely to be familiar with criminals, than the honest animals. All the other moles I knew were part of organised warfare, undermining everyone with their tunnels, so they seemed to be a good starting point. My plan would have been more effective if they actually knew any hedgehogs at all.

Then we ran into another red squirrel, so Squirrel tried a different approach.

"Hello. Excuse me. I wondered…" But, before she'd even finished, the other squirrel had run off into the trees.

Eventually we found a deer and tried a rather less direct method.

"Hello, I'm Alfie Dog and this is Squirrel and Rabbit. You've got a lovely wood here. It's quite similar to our wood, you may know it, it's the one past the road of cherry trees?"

"Ah yes. I know that area. I do go over there occasionally."

Then before I could even think of what to say next, he carried on.

"I have heard that the fraudster Hedgehog is due for release soon. I should watch what you leave lying around."

"Oh," Squirrel said, "is he very bad?"

"Well," said the deer, "I heard he stole an awful lot of things from an awful lot of animals. There's a plot going on amongst some of the animals to recover what they lost. That's all I'll say."

I saw an opportunity. "I heard he had a letter from a distant cousin. Is that something to do with it?"

The deer laughed. "Oh yes, it wasn't from a Hedgehog at all, it was one of our woodland mice in disguise in the photograph they sent him. I have to say in costume he didn't look too bad."

We chatted away for a while and laughed about the 'clever plan' before I said I'd better find the Boss before she went without us. We said goodbye to the deer and headed back to the car.

"How are you going to break the news to Hedgehog?" Rabbit asked.

"I don't know. Our first problem is how we get all of us back into the car. When the door opens, I'll create another diversion then you two run in before I get in. As soon as I'm in the Boss will close the door."

"Right," Rabbit said. "Are you ready, Squirrel?"

"I think so."

They ran to hide behind the nearest tree until I gave the signal.

As we went towards the car, I looked out for something to point out to distract the Boss but there weren't many people around that part of the park. It was going to be tricky. She opened the door and I pulled away suddenly in the opposite direction.

"Oh, Alfie, will you come here." The Boss had turned back towards the car.

I was just in time to see Squirrel clamber over the entrance and Rabbit quickly hiding under the car.

"Alfie, will you please get into the car?"

I wasn't sure how I could delay any more. What about Rabbit? How was I going to get him into the car? The door closed behind me and there was no sign of rabbit. I could feel Squirrel wriggling under the blanket as I sat up to peer out of the window. As I looked back, I could see Rabbit running after us and waving. I didn't know what to do. Perhaps now was the time to tell the Boss the whole story and get her to go back for Rabbit. We couldn't just leave him there. I had another idea. "Excuse me," I shouted above the noise of the engine. "Could we stop just a minute? I really need the toilet."

"Oh, Alfie, you've had all that time at the park why didn't you think to go then?"

"Sorry," I muttered as she pulled the car in between some parked cars and came to open the door for me.

"Now hurry up."

I did my usual sniffing the ground thing playing for time so that Rabbit could catch up. I could see him in the distance puffing and panting. Fortunately, the door had been left open for me and as soon as I'd seen Rabbit jump over the step, I got back in and sat down. I could hear Rabbit panting and began to pant myself to cover the noise.

"Are you all right?"

"Yes sorry," I said. "I'll be ok in a minute," and at last we settled down for the journey home.

As soon as I got an opportunity, I went down to the woods in search of Squirrel and Rabbit. "Oh, Rabbit, I thought you were never going to make it."

"I wouldn't have fancied your chances of explaining that one to my Mum." He laughed.

"I don't fancy having to break this news to Hedgehog either. I'm glad you're going to be there, Squirrel. I don't suppose you want to come too, do you Rabbit?"

"Sorry, mate. I'm not setting foot in that prison. No fear."

On the way to the prison, Squirrel and I rehearsed how

we would tell Hedgehog that he really didn't have a cousin after all. We decided that as I knew Hedgehog better I should be the one to tell him. I couldn't help thinking that Squirrel might do a better job, I was worried I would blurt it out rather than say what we agreed. Squirrel went through it with me several times, as we walked along, but even she concluded there wasn't an easy way to break news like that. He was an 'orphan hedgehog'. He would have loved to find he had some real live relatives somewhere.

By the time we were led in to see Hedgehog I had rehearsed my speech so many times in my head. My nose was dry and my paws felt decidedly sweaty. As we approached the table, instead of saying hello, I immediately said, "I'm really sorry Hedgehog he isn't your cousin. The deer said he's a woodland mouse in disguise. They want to get their own back on you and they are all ganging up to get some money back and they think you stole lots of things from them and they don't know what a nice person you are and..."

"Alfie, sit down," said Hedgehog. "It's all right, really. It was what I was expecting." Fortunately, Hedgehog put his paw on my arm and stopped me; otherwise I might have gone on blurting all day. Hedgehog smiled a sad smile and said again that he suspected something along those lines. He also said they were right to be annoyed with him and maybe when he was released we could go to see them together and he could try to make up for some of the bad things he did when he was younger. Then he got the photo out again and we all had a good chuckle at the mouse dressed up as a hedgehog. If you looked very closely, you could see some of his whiskers poking out, but because we hadn't suspected it was a mouse before, we hadn't been looking for them.

Of course, Hedgehog was disappointed that he didn't have any relatives, but as he said, "I've got you two and that's more than I have ever had before."

With only a couple more weeks until Hedgehog came out of prison, I wanted to make the most of the time I could spend with Squirrel. "Now the weather is better, would you like to come for a picnic." I felt almost as nervous as the first time I'd been to see Hedgehog.

Squirrel jumped up and down with delight. "Oh Alfie, I just love picnics. When can we go?"

"Thursday," I said. Although I could have said Wednesday or Friday as I wasn't doing anything on those days either, but I liked the sound of Thursday.

When the day of the picnic arrived, I went to prepare the food. I'd watched the Boss making sandwiches, so I had a fair idea of what to do and it was amazing what I could find in the kitchen cupboards by having a good rummage. I made a bit of a mess in the kitchen, but I was sure the Boss wouldn't mind clearing up when I'd finished.

I found the marzipan for pudding and all different types of meat. I had some difficulty using the knife to spread the butter so resorted to using my paw in the end. It didn't give such an even spread, but I was sure Squirrel would understand.

"Alfie, you really can't take all of those things on a picnic." The Boss was surveying the mess that had previously been the kitchen.

"Why not?"

"Well for a start you won't be able to carry them. Then you haven't got anything to cook them on, and besides, you don't know how to cook some of them."

"I can eat the steak raw," I said, horrified that I might find myself with nothing more exciting than dog food.

"You can take the cooked chicken leg, but be careful with the bone. One bar of marzipan, you really can't take all five bars and just one of the bags of crisps. Have you fetched some of the nuts out of the other cupboard for Squirrel?"

I trotted through to the cupboard where the bird food lived. "Can I take some dog biscuits and begging strips, just in case I run out of everything else?"

A firm, "No, Alfie, you've got quite enough," came back from the other room.

Then I folded up one of my blankets to sit on and was ready with the hamper. It was a beautiful day, but as it was quite difficult balancing the hamper and the blanket, I made slow progress into the wood to find Squirrel. I dropped the picnic hamper once or twice and was worried that the crisps would end up as thousands of crumbs, but who was I kidding, I would enjoy eating them just the same.

Squirrel was ready and waiting when I arrived and was carrying a tiny parasol to provide shade from the sun.

We headed off to the farthest end of the woods away from everyday life and the animals we knew. There was a little stream with grassy banks, where sometimes I walked with the Boss and where we never saw another person. This, I decided, would be the ideal spot for a picnic. I set the hamper down and stretched out in the sun. It was perfect and we talked and laughed and played. I did quite a lot of talking, to make up for the time I had the picnic hamper in my mouth. We almost forgot to eat the food, but I didn't want to have to carry it home again. As squirrel was getting too hot, we moved to a spot that was partly in shade and I got out the picnic. I unfolded the cloth and laid it on the centre of the blanket. I then took out a glass for squirrel and a bowl for me and some plastic plates. Squirrel thought the plates were funny. Animals don't normally worry about dropping crumbs. We had some difficulty balancing the plates on our paws whilst we ate, but we had fun trying. Squirrel had to help me with the corkscrew.

Squirrel watched as I took out all the packages of food from the hamper and put them on the cloth.

"Oh, Alfie you've thought of everything," she said as I put the little salt and pepper pots down next to the chicken.

I smiled in delight, I hadn't actually thought of very much at all, the Boss had helped.

Squirrel raised her glass and clinked it against my bowl. "A toast to friends," and I readily agreed.

It was a wonderful lazy afternoon and I didn't want it to come to an end. Eventually it became a little cooler and we began to pack up before it started to get dark.

"I've had a lovely day," I said to Squirrel. "Can we do this again sometime?"

"I'd love to," she said, in a gentle voice.

I couldn't have been a happier dog.

CHAPTER 10
THE PLANNING MEETING

Before I knew where we were, it was time for the Woodland Council meeting to consider our plans. I was excited and nervous all rolled into one. I wanted to find out the decision on the same day as the meeting, but the only way to do that would be to find someone to ask when the meeting finished. The main problem with that idea was that with the Security Buzzard, I just couldn't get anywhere near the place. I decided that I'd get as close as I could to the meeting, but I didn't want to get into trouble. If only I was born with a little more patience, like Squirrel, or a little more bravado, like Rabbit.

"I won't just stand around waiting if you don't mind." Squirrel patted my arm. "I'm too nervous and with you running around in circles it's just making me worse."

"I intend to be happy whatever the outcome."

"You don't believe that really, do you?" she asked.

"No, I suppose not. I'll see you later."

I waited on my own, but the meeting was long and it started to get dark. I decided I had no choice but to go home and wait to find out the following morning.

Early next day Squirrel was already up when I arrived at her house.

She closed the front door and joined me. "I think the best way to find out would be to see PC Badger. He always seems to know what's going on in the wood."

Having had previous encounters with the Police

Badger, I wasn't all that keen, but I wanted to know the outcome so I agreed.

I knocked at the door of the Woodland Police Station. "Excuse me," I called very hesitantly. "Is there anybody in?"

"Morning, young Alfie." PC Badger's voice made me jump. "How can I help you?"

I immediately wished I hadn't come. "We, well that is to say, I was just wondering. But if it's too much trouble. I'll just…" And I turned to start walking down the path, back the way I'd come.

"Now there's nothing to be concerned about, young Alfie. As long as you haven't been eating any more acorns." The badger chuckled.

"How did you know?" I asked without thinking about what I was saying and for a moment, feeling very alarmed.

"It's my job to know what's going on in the woods. Besides, I noticed that you became friends with Squirrel. Then I thought to myself 'Why would a young puppy make friends with a squirrel?' And then I thought to myself 'acorns'. There you are, Alfie, that's the power of deduction at work."

"Wow. That's amazing. I'm not actually supposed to eat acorns as it turns out, so I leave that bit to Squirrel now." By this time, I'd quite forgotten that I'd come to see Badger about something.

"Now what was it you wanted, young chap?" said Badger as kindly as I'd ever heard him speak.

"Oh, yes. I was just wondering whether you knew the results from the Planning Meeting last night. I'm so eager to hear about my den."

"I'm afraid I can't answer that one. That's official business and you have to find out from the Council Notice.

If you go along to the Forest Notice Board at eleven this morning you'll be able to see it with all the other applicants."

"Thank you, sir." I didn't really knowing what else to say. Then having nothing better to do for the next three hours, I went back to see if Squirrel or Rabbit wanted to join me sitting by the notice board until the results were posted up. I couldn't find Rabbit but Squirrel said she would come.

I was feeling more and more nervous as time passed. We played 'I Spy' for about half an hour before Squirrel said she really couldn't stand playing it for even one more time and asked me if there was any chance I could stop pacing up and down as it was starting to make her feel nervous as well.

"Oh dear, Squirrel, I just don't know what to think. On the one paw if I get the go ahead I have to start getting the work done, which is going to be very expensive and very difficult. On the other paw, if I get turned down I just don't know what I'll do. The worst part would be how would I tell Hedgehog? Do you think if that happened, maybe you could tell him for me?" I looked at Squirrel making my puppy dog eyes as big as possible.

Squirrel glared at me. "You know, those eyes really don't work on me. If you don't get permission I really think it should be you who tells Hedgehog. You are his friend after all."

"Oh dear, I thought as much." I started pacing again.

Through gritted teeth, Squirrel said, "If you don't stop pacing I'm going home and leaving you to get the result on your own."

"Oh sorry." I flopped down on the ground. I played with a stick, chewing one end and then using it as a paint-brush to draw pictures. After about five minutes, everything was proving too much and I got up to chase my tail for a few minutes.

"Ok. That's enough, I'm going home. Come and tell me what the result is when you know." And before I could object she had run off up a tree to take the shortcut.

It wasn't much longer before other animals started to turn up, all wanting to be first to see the result of their own applications. There were field mice and rabbits, moles and wood pigeons, all pushing and shoving. There was so much excitement and chatter and I introduced myself to any of the animals that didn't feel the need to sit as far away from me as possible.

When eleven o' clock arrived, a stoat, who worked for the council, pushed his way through the throng of animals. "Come on," he shouted, "If you don't let me through you're never going to know if you've been successful."

We moved aside to make a pathway to the board. There were three sheets of paper and as soon as he had pinned them up and moved away we all started jostling for position. The smaller animals found it easiest to get to the front and the birds flew up and landed on the heads of the animals nearest the board. There were little whoops and tweets of joy as one after another, each animal found that their application had been successful. A crow came away muttering that he couldn't see why he needed to provide 'ground access' to his plot and complaining that it was going to add to the cost, but on the whole the animals seemed to be happy.

Despite having been the first one there, I was struggling to get to the board. I thought of barking to frighten the others out of the way, but if I was going to live in the wood, these were going to be my neighbours, so it might not be such a good idea. At last, I worked my way to the front and there it was, 'Application by Alfie Dog,' I looked along the line to see the result, 'DECLINED'. It must be a mistake. I must have read the wrong line. I lifted my paw up to the board and traced the line carefully from my name. It still said 'DECLINED'. I moved my paw along to the reason given, where it simply said 'Not a necessary dwelling'.

I flopped down to the ground and beat my paws against the soil. I was feeling utterly deflated. What was I going to do? More to the point, what was Hedgehog going to do? It was only a week until he would be out of prison; he couldn't just live in the pile of leaves in the garden forever.

"You can resubmit your application," said one of the deer kindly. "If you make some changes, I'm sure they'll let it through eventually."

"Thanks." I didn't look up. "I'll do that."

I must have sat there for another twenty minutes before a little voice at my side said, "I wondered why you hadn't come back. I'm sorry I got annoyed earlier."

"Oh, Squirrel," I sobbed, letting all the emotion catch up with me. "It really wasn't that. I do know I can be annoying. I annoy myself too. I'm still here because we didn't get it and I didn't know how to tell you. All your hard work and we didn't get it."

As I continued to sob, Squirrel took out her little handkerchief and started to wipe away my tears.

"Oh, Alfie, dear, I'm so sorry. I know how much it meant to you." Then she sat resting her paw on mine as I continued to cry.

"What are we going to do if Hedgehog goes back to a life of crime because his hope has gone?" I sniffed through my tears.

"Alfie," said Squirrel, "we are his hope, not the den. It's having friends that has really made the difference."

"Oh, I do hope you're right." I went back to sniffling into the handkerchief. "It isn't as though we can afford to keep resubmitting the plans, only to have them rejected." By now, Squirrel had tears in her eyes too and I suddenly forgot my own sadness and felt the need to put my arm around Squirrel to cheer her up. Squirrel nestled into my shoulder and as I wiped away my own tears, I tried to sound bright for her sake. "We'll sort it out somehow. It isn't the end of the world." And as I said it, I almost started to believe that it was true. I wished I hadn't already soaked her handkerchief through and that I had something to dry her eyes with.

We were quiet for a while and then I said, "How am I going to tell Hedgehog?"

"I don't know." Squirrel looked at me very sadly.

We both knew how much it meant to him. "I wondered whether to play it down and say that with a few revisions I think we'll get it through next time or whether to be completely honest and say I don't think we stand a hope. What do you think?"

"I don't know," she said again. "Whatever you say, he isn't going to like it. What I do know is that it's important to be honest with him."

"I know it wouldn't be the same, but I suppose I could build a den in the garden at home. It wouldn't have the same feeling, but it might be better than nothing."

"Could we still have the acorn catcher?" asked Squirrel.

"Only if I can find an oak tree to build it around." We set off home in search of an oak tree in the garden.

By bedtime, we had found that there weren't any suitable oak trees in the garden so even if we built the den, there would be no point in adding the acorn catcher. By this time Squirrel seemed much brighter. But then, she already had a little home of her own.

I didn't sleep well that night. I was tossing and turning. How would I break the news to Hedgehog? I could write him a letter and not see him at all, but that didn't seem quite right. I spent the next morning making sure that the pile of leaves I'd offered Hedgehog was nice and big and protected from the surrounding area. It wasn't going to be nearly so much fun for him, without a fireside to sit next to in the winter.

I really wanted to get the bad news out of the way and then be able to start looking forward to Hedgehog's release next week. The whole den idea was hanging like a cloud. I went off into the forest to clear my head and work out what to say. I bumped into Rabbit.

"Hi, Alfie. I'm sorry your den was turned down. It sounded fun."

"Thanks. It's ok. It was just a den to me, but it was going to be home for Hedgehog. After all the years of being passed from pillar to post, Hedgehog was finally going to settle down and start a new life."

"Mum said she'd heard that's why it was turned down." Rabbit tried to stifle a bounce.

"What?" I was suddenly angry. "How could the Woodland Council be so mean?"

"I think the Woodland Council was hoping Hedgehog would move as far away as possible, they don't seem to like trouble makers." He grinned.

"But how is a chap to start again without any support and encouragement?" I asked feeling indignant. "Ok, so I'm just a puppy and maybe I'll turn out to be wrong, but I actually believe that Hedgehog regrets how his life has been and really wants to make amends."

"Well who knows?" Rabbit said. "I think he sounds

rather fun to have around, but don't tell my mum I said that."

CHAPTER 11
BREAKING THE NEWS TO HEDGEHOG

I woke early and was feeling very nervous. I marched up and down saying to myself, "I can do it. I can do it. Hedgehog is my friend. This isn't about the den. It's about being his friend." Then I marched up and down saying, "I can't do it. I can't do it. I wish Squirrel were coming with me. I wish Squirrel had agreed to tell him. She would have been so much better at it than I will be." Then I repeated the exercise several times and made myself finish on a chorus of, "I can do it, I can do it." I did this in the hope that it might make a difference.

I got to the prison gates for the start of visiting, to give myself as long as possible with Hedgehog. A weasel led me through to the visiting room and I took my seat. Hedgehog came through looking eager for news. I just sat there, opening and closing my mouth like a goldfish, but nothing coming out. Hedgehog just sat there too and waited for me to talk.

There was a long awkward silence until eventually Hedgehog said, "Are you trying to tell me something, young Alfie?"

I felt annoyed. "I would have thought that was obvious."

"Now there's no need to be rude. I was trying to make it easy for you." Hedgehog took hold of the edge of the table with his paws.

"Easy for me, how can you make it easier for me? It's all your fault there isn't going to be a den. It's been refused because none of the animals want to live near you in the forest." I clasped my paws over my mouth in horror. As soon as it was out, I realised what a dreadful thing I'd done and desperately started to say I was sorry.

Hedgehog had got up, and with tears in his eyes quietly said, "I thought you knew me better than that. I really thought you were my friend." Then he slowly walked away from the table with his shoulders slumped.

"Don't go," I called. "I didn't mean it. I'm sorry. I'm really sorry. It wasn't meant to come out like that. I don't care what the other animals think. I am your friend." But the problem was, that in that moment I had meant it and Hedgehog must have known that his battle to start again was almost impossible.

I had never felt so lonely as I walked away from the prison. I knew I'd let myself down and I hated the feeling. What was I going to do? For a start, I'd have to see Squirrel and whatever would she think of me for the way I'd behaved. It was unforgivable.

Then I thought sadly that in a few days Hedgehog would come out of prison and I needed to make all the arrangements with him. I hadn't even told him that I'd made sure there was a lovely big pile of leaves in the corner of the garden and that I'd even asked The Boss if the leaves could stay there for a while, until we sorted something else out. Oh, how could I be such a stupid puppy? I didn't really blame Hedgehog at all. It wasn't his fault that the Woodland Council were so short-sighted and horrible.

Somehow, I had to sort this mess out and do it quickly. I remembered to ask the weasels what time Hedgehog would be allowed out on Wednesday and they said they thought it would be about 3.00 in the afternoon. All I could do was make sure I was there waiting and be ready to apologise. I wondered if I should try to write to Hedgehog in the meantime.

The following day I pulled myself together enough to see Squirrel. I wanted nothing more than for Squirrel to shout at me. That would have made it all feel a lot easier.

"Oh, Squirrel, yesterday didn't go well. My visit to Hedgehog was nothing short of a disaster. I so wish you'd gone with me. You're so much more sensitive than I am and you always seem to know the right thing to say in bad situations. I just blunder on. I expected I'd do my normal thing of just blurting it all out and hardly stopping for breath, but I tried desperately to prepare the right wording. I really did try hard."

When Squirrel could get a word in edgeways, she asked me to tell her exactly what had happened. Then when I'd finished, she didn't shout at me or even raise her voice, she just put her arm around as much of my neck as she could get it round and said, "There, there, Alfie. I know it's hard. I know how disappointed you are and hopefully Hedgehog will understand that too."

It just made me feel much worse; it wasn't just how I felt that mattered in all this. I sloped off into the woods to write a letter to Hedgehog. I could at least try getting it to him before he came out of prison.

This is what I wrote.

"My dearest Hedgehog,

I am so ashamed of the way I behaved on Saturday. I am very very sorry. I am disappointed that our planning application was turned down, more because it was such an important step in your life, than for anything for me. I simply didn't know how to tell you, as I realised how disappointed you would be.

Please find it in your heart to forgive me. I still have so much to learn. Your friendship is as important to me as mine is to you. I'm sure that if we work together we can find some way of making the Woodland Council change its mind. I will be waiting by the prison gates for you at 3.00 on the third of May. I have prepared a lovely pile of leaves for you to live in, in the corner of the garden and The Boss has promised that no one will disturb them. Please come home with me.

Your ever faithful friend
Alfie"

Once I finished writing it, I went to find the nearest magpie to send it first class post. I marked the envelope 'urgent' and put a note saying there was nothing valuable or shiny inside and sent it on its way.

I was sitting kicking my heels, wondering what to do next, when Rabbit came along. His head was down and he wasn't bouncing. "Sorry," he said. "Squirrel told me what happened and I just wanted to say sorry. I should never have told you what Mum said. I hope you sort things out with Hedgehog. If I can help in any way."

I'd never seen Rabbit like that, I didn't know what to say. "Thanks, Rabbit. I'll let you know."

Wednesday finally arrived, the day when Hedgehog was to be released from prison. Regardless of whether he had received the letter, Squirrel and I packed some sandwiches and waited at the gates from midday, to be in plenty of time to welcome him. The leaves were ready for his arrival and everything was in order. I just hoped that by later in the day, Hedgehog would move in.

We didn't talk much as we stood at the prison gates. We both felt worried about what was going to happen. By 2.30pm, we were getting very fidgety and I was trying desperately not to pace up and down or chase my tail, as the last thing I wanted was for Squirrel to go home and leave me waiting alone. 3.00pm came and went and there was no sign of Hedgehog. By 4.00pm, we were wondering what was going on, so I rang the bell and spoke to one of the weasels.

"Excuse me."

"Yes," said the weasel abruptly.

"Squirrel and I were wondering what time Hedgehog is being released?"

At the mention of Squirrel, the weasel softened and in a more friendly tone said, "I'm sorry, he was released at 10.00 this morning and he immediately ambled away into the undergrowth."

"I'm sorry to bother you, but do you happen to know if he received my letter before he was released," I asked.

"I'll find out for you." The weasel went off to ask one of his colleagues and when he came back, he had the unopened letter in his paw. It had been given to Hedgehog, but he had left it behind in his cell. We didn't know what to do next and then the guard, still being really helpful, said, "You could try tracking him. After all he can't walk as fast as you, so you should be able to catch up with him quite easily."

"That's a great idea, thank you. The first problem I can think of though is that I don't have anything with his scent on to follow."

The guard went to see if they still had anything

belonging to Hedgehog. When he came back, he said, "I'm sorry he's taken the few things he had with him. Your best bet would be to sniff his old cell. It hasn't been cleaned yet. If you'll come this way, I'll take you through."

I left Squirrel at the gates and followed the weasel into the prison, for what I hoped would be the last occasion. This time we went past the interview room and into the main prison itself. Having the door locked behind me was a very scary feeling and I really wasn't at all happy about it. Hedgehog's cell was quite small and had a tiny window high up in the wall. There were no leaves to make it cosy, just some twigs for a bed and a small table with a desk lamp. I shuddered at the thought of spending months of my life shut up somewhere like this and regretted even more the things I'd said to Hedgehog the other day.

I pulled myself together, had a good sniff round Hedgehog's cell and was happy that I really had Hedgehog's scent. Then I headed back to Squirrel and freedom. I was ready for the hard work to begin.

"Now," I said to Squirrel, as I took a deep breath, "I have a very important job to do." Whilst tracking things by smell, as a game, is fun and it doesn't matter if I got it wrong, this was different. This time I had to do it for real and if I made a mistake, no one was going to say, "No, left a bit. Yes, you're getting warmer," and give me clues. I wasn't sure that I was going to be very good at it. One thing was certain, I owed it to Hedgehog to do my best.

I found the path Hedgehog had taken on leaving the prison, but it wasn't long before he left the path and went off into the undergrowth. It was a slow process to work my way through the wood. I was prickled by brambles, stung by nettles and had to keep reminding myself that it was my own fault in the first place. Squirrel stayed in the trees just above me, giving me an idea of what lay ahead.

I kept my nose to the ground, desperate not to lose the scent. The path that hedgehog took was in exactly the opposite direction to where I lived. It was clear he had no intention of coming to find us, which made me feel very sad. It was getting dark and we were tired, so we marked the spot where we were and went home for the night.

"I know that scent isn't visible, even in the light," I said, "but it's much harder to sniff when I can't see where I'm going and I'm a little bit scared too."

"That's ok," said Squirrel. "I'm sure we'll do much better tomorrow, after a good night's sleep."

CHAPTER 12
THE SEARCH FOR HEDGEHOG

As it turned out, neither Squirrel nor I slept well. When we met the following morning, we didn't feel refreshed or talkative. I was worried we'd lose the scent and that the more time passed, the harder it was going to be to track Hedgehog. Whatever happened, I had to find him. We met Rabbit on the way to continuing the search.

"Yo, dudes." Rabbit was carrying an American comic that he'd found blowing about in the woods. He'd obviously been reading it.

"Look," said Squirrel staring at the floor. "I know I don't always approve of your games, but will you help us?"

"Really? Me? No one ever asks me to help. It's usually 'you're in the way again, Rabbit', 'Go and play outside and give me some peace, Rabbit.' Never 'Do you think you could help me with this, Rabbit?' I'd love to, but please, my mum mustn't know what I'm doing. I don't think she'd approve."

I crossed my fingers that Rabbit wouldn't get up to his usual mischief and we set off. "Ok," Rabbit said, bouncing ahead. "Where do we start?"

"We marked the spot we got to last night," I said. "Follow me." I snuffled around trying to get a scent with Rabbit copying me snuffling behind. I stopped and Rabbit piled into me and we landed in a heap.

"Rabbit!" Squirrel shook her head.

"Ok, ok, I'm with the programme." Rabbit stepped back

and kicked a stone.

"You're welcome to sniff, just not so close. You're putting me off."

"Ok, bro, you got it."

Squirrel rolled her eyes.

We had a couple of false starts when I thought I was following Hedgehog, then ended up in a dead end and had to go back and start again.

"I don't smell nothing," Rabbit said.

"That would mean you do smell something," Squirrel said quietly.

"No. I really don't."

"Rabbit, just leave the sniffing to Alfie. You can help keep the path clear for him."

"I'm onto it, sis."

"Rabbit, I am not your sis, your sister or any other such term. Now just settle down." I could see Squirrel's hair raised on the back of her neck and I for one had no plan to argue with her.

Eventually I found the trail heading away from our wood and towards the main road. I'd been there with the Boss, but we never actually crossed the road. It was a road with lots of lorries and as Hedgehog was quite slow I became worried in case he hadn't made it safely to the other side.

When we got to the road, I told the others to sit down and look both ways, to make sure it was safe to cross. We all sat in a line. It must have looked quite a funny sight, a dog, a squirrel and a rabbit all sitting at the side of the road waiting for a gap in the traffic, but eventually it was safe and we went over to the other side. The Boss would have been proud of me, although that may have been after being cross with me for going out on my own.

I couldn't follow Hedgehog's scent as we crossed the road, so when we got to the other side it took quite a while to pick up the trail, but I got it in the end.

We kept going until mid-afternoon. Then Rabbit said, "I'm having fun, but I have to go before my Mum sends out a search party for me. Or worse, she might send PC Badger."

We all laughed. "We'll let you know how we get on." I waved him off. We had gone back to the road with him to make sure he got across all right and then got back to work.

"You have to admit he has been helpful," I said to Squirrel.

"Eventually." She smiled.

I followed the scent a bit further, but it was fading fast and we were now starting to struggle.

Squirrel put her paw gently on my arm. "Why don't we try to get as big a search party as we can muster and try again tomorrow?"

I didn't want to let Hedgehog down, but I was so tired, I couldn't carry on as I was. I knew Squirrel was right, I just hoped that the following day wasn't going to be too late. I also hoped there were some animals who would be willing to help.

As we went back through the wood, we called on everyone we knew to ask if they would help. "Please can you join us to search for Hedgehog tomorrow? When he left prison he wandered off because he thought that nobody cared about him."

"Hedgehog had a hard life, he wants to make amends, but he's missing. Please can you help?"

We talked to every animal we could find as we worked our way through the forest. "We're meeting on the edge of the wood tomorrow morning at seven. Everyone deserves a second chance, please help."

We were met by grunts and moans from animals who had lost money at the hands of Hedgehog and others who were uncertain of our motives. As we headed home exhausted all we could do was hope.

By Friday, it had been two days since Hedgehog's release from prison. Even allowing for how slowly he moved he could have gone quite a distance in that time. It was a fine day and I hoped the weather would hold. We stood a much better chance of finding him in good weather. I was early calling for Squirrel and with both of us having slept a little better we felt brighter and more optimistic.

"Do you think there will be at least one or two animals turning out to help us?" I asked.

"I'm hoping so," said Squirrel. "There are a few who may come as a favour and I'm sure Rabbit will be there." She grinned at me and I nodded.

"As long as his mother lets him." I laughed.

We walked slowly towards the edge of the wood hoping to be met by some of the other animals, although deep down, both of us weren't really expecting anyone to turn out for Hedgehog.

It may have been because we cared so much whether Hedgehog was all right. It may have been because I explained the story of how Hedgehog hadn't had much chance when he was small. It may have been saying how he wanted to put things right, but as we turned the last corner, there they all were, dozens of animals ready and waiting to join us in the search. There were Rabbit and his mum and brother, and one of the magpies and Police Badger out of uniform and three of the deer and one of the prison warder weasels in his civilian clothes and so many others that I couldn't count them all. I just stood there speechless. Squirrel had tears rolling down her face. It was amazing.

Eventually, I thanked them all for coming and explained that as the scent was getting cold, it was going to mean more of a search than a sniff. I led them all to the road and we all crossed carefully, before going into the wood on the other side. No one was there to see a whole forest of animals checking to make sure the road was clear before crossing.

We all spread out in a line across the wood and started working our way forwards. We moved very slowly, inching paw by paw through the woods. Everyone was silent as they searched.

"Hey," called one of the deer. "I've found a big pile of leaves here. Could this be him?"

I rushed over and sniffed, but there was no sign of Hedgehog and from the way the leaves were pulled together, I suspected that someone had been gathering them up, but I was sure it wasn't Hedgehog.

"Should we just move them aside to make sure?" The deer seemed disappointed that he hadn't been the one to find Hedgehog.

"Yes, that's probably a good idea." I gently prodded the pile with my paw. Then from nowhere, Rabbit bounced into the middle of the pile, sending leaves up in all directions.

"Rabbit!" Squirrel shouted. "What if he'd been underneath?"

"I'd have been prickled?"

"And you could have hurt Hedgehog."

"Sorry," Rabbit said and bounced back to his place in the line.

We all continued to shuffle forwards. It took about

three hours before I heard a shout from Rabbit further along to the left. "I know you won't believe this, but I think I've found him." We all stopped and went over to where Rabbit was standing.

There was a pile of leaves at the foot of a big cedar tree with a little notice next to a makeshift front door saying 'Do Not Disturb'. I sniffed around and sure enough, it smelled of Hedgehog. I called "Hedgehog," but there was no answer, so I called again. We heard some rustling and I realised that I could just make out a little eye looking at me through the leaves. I cleared my throat and gave a little speech. "Hedgehog, well obviously the first thing I need to say is sorry, but then," and I continued really excitedly, "all the animals here today want you to come back to live in our wood and they all want you to have a chance of a new life and to be your neighbours and your friends. We've spent the last three days looking for you and we're so glad we've found you. Please come out to see us."

Nothing happened.

Squirrel nudged me. "Maybe it will take a bit of time for it to sink in. Why don't you leave the letter for him and say we'll come back tomorrow?" So that's exactly what we did.

I thanked all the other animals as we walked back together through the woods. In turn, they tried to reassure me that everything would be ok and Rabbit who was in high spirits, asked if he could come with us tomorrow, which was lovely. Even though we hadn't got Hedgehog to come home, we had done everything we possibly could and we were thrilled by the response from all the animals around the wood. Squirrel had even told Rabbit how well he'd done.

CHAPTER 13
HEDGEHOG HAS GONE

It was early on Saturday morning when I called for Squirrel. I couldn't wait to see if Hedgehog had forgiven me. When I got to Squirrel's house, Rabbit was already there and seemed to be at least as excited as I was. It felt good to have Rabbit with us. I didn't mind that I hadn't got Squirrel all to myself, I felt it was important to show Hedgehog that there were more animals who cared about him and wanted him to stay, even if Hedgehog had warned me not to spend time with Rabbit. This time, because we knew where Hedgehog was, it didn't take us long to find him. At least, it didn't take us long to find the spot where he had been yesterday.

Once we crossed the main road, we arrived at the cedar tree in next to no time. We were certain that it was the same cedar tree, but the notice had gone, the leaves had been spread around and there was no sign of Hedgehog anywhere. I wanted to start looking for him all over again and had already sniffed to see which way the scent went before Squirrel managed to take my paw very gently in hers.

"You're going to have to leave it, Alfie. The letter has gone. We need to let Hedgehog make his own decisions."

"But, but anything could happen to him. What if he gets lost or…"

"Alfie, he won't get lost. We'd better go home." Squirrel tried to lead me away.

I took my paw away. "You go. I'm going to stay here for a while in case he comes back."

"Alfie," said Squirrel again, "he isn't coming back. You can see he's tidied the place up, so it hardly looks as though he was ever here at all. You've tried. You've really tried. Come home with me and Rabbit."

"I'll wait too." Rabbit kicked some leaves.

I shook my head. "I'm just going to stay here for a little while. I'd like to be on my own anyway."

Reluctant as they were, Squirrel and Rabbit started to head back.

I stayed in the far wood for quite some time before trudging home feeling very sad and miserable. When I got home, I sat in one spot, then got up and moved to another, then I moved again, wandering round the house feeling lost. I went out of the back door only when I absolutely needed to and spent the rest of the time curled up in my bed fidgeting. It wasn't until the afternoon that I opened the front door, to see if I was missing anything. As it turned out, I was missing quite a lot. There on the doorstep was Hedgehog looking all dishevelled, with a little bag of his belongings.

"I thought you were never going to open it," he said. "I've been standing here for four hours, what with not being able to reach the bell."

"Oh, Hedgehog, I'm so pleased to see you. I thought you'd left us completely." I hugged Hedgehog as best you can hug a prickly animal without getting hurt. "Come with me, let me show you the pile of leaves I've got ready for you." And we wandered down the garden to the corner I had prepared. "You know I really am sorry," I said, "and I will do anything I can to make things up to you."

"It's ok," he said. "I've been thinking about it and I

understand. I would probably have reacted the same way, if it had been the other way around. But tell me, all those other animals who came with you, are they really willing to give me a second chance?"

I nodded and told him about my little speech.

"Thank you," he said quietly. "That means a great deal to me."

Then Hedgehog nodded his approval at the pile of leaves and my tail couldn't stop wagging with delight.

"You know, Alfie, when you came to find me yesterday, I was already on my way back to find you. It's not so easy for me, I don't walk as quickly as you do. It had already taken me a long time to get to where I was and I get tired when I walk all the time. I waited until night time to cross the road to make sure it was not so busy and then walked through this wood on Saturday. I was starting to think I was going to have to stand on the doorstep all day. One thing I realised as I did all that walking, was that it wasn't really you I was running away from. I was trying to run away from myself. I know how hard it's going to be and how many times there will be people against me. I guess I just thought I wasn't strong enough to do it on my own. When you turned up with all those animals, I realised I didn't have to do it on my own. I need your help. I need your friendship. Don't let us ever have cross words again."

All I could do was nod. I was too choked up to say anything. We just sat together in silence for a while, but it was a companionable happy silence and we both knew we would always help each other, no matter how hard it was or how much opposition we faced.

Eventually, Hedgehog said, "Well I'd better get myself cleaned up and I could do with some food."

I went to get the food, whilst Hedgehog had a wash and

settled into his new quarters. He put the letter that I'd written to him in pride of place on the mantelpiece, as a constant reminder of the importance of our friendship. Amongst the few meagre belongings Hedgehog had, it was his most treasured possession. Then when he had eaten and recovered from his journey, we set off for Squirrel's house to give her the good news. Hedgehog travelled on my back to save his little legs from any more walking.

It was gone 5.00pm when we came out of Squirrel's house to head home and there outside Squirrel's oak tree were the other animals, with a big banner saying 'welcome home' and they all shouted "Surprise," and began a party to celebrate. Neither I nor Hedgehog had any idea how the news had spread so quickly, although I suspected it might have had something to do with the buzzard who was holding one end of the banner and Rabbit was looking particularly pleased with himself.

Hedgehog was utterly overwhelmed by his complete change in fortune and gave a little speech to thank everyone and say that he promised that we would not be disappointed and he was going to devote his life to making up for the bad things he'd done.

As we walked home later, Hedgehog said he thought he might just have an idea. He wouldn't tell me what it was, he said he wanted to sleep on it and maybe he would share the whole thing with me in the morning. I was excited just by the thought of an idea, even though I couldn't guess whether it was a good one or not.

On Monday, I took some breakfast, on a tray, down to Hedgehog. It had all been neatly laid out when I set off along the path, but in my usual fashion, it was not quite so neat by the time I arrived. I had walked very slowly down the garden, but the emphasis should have been on carefully. As it turned out Hedgehog quite liked yoghurt, but wasn't so keen on Frosties, which was a great relief to me as it meant I could eat those. I'd already stopped and eaten the ones that had fallen off the tray on route, but I was more than happy to finish the rest.

"You'll have to wait to hear my idea until Squirrel comes round," Hedgehog said as he ate the last of the yoghurt.

"Do you think we should include Rabbit too?" I asked.

"Well." Hedgehog rubbed his chin and smiled. "Perhaps being involved with this is just what Rabbit needs."

"I'll go and find him." I ran off into the wood. "Rabbit, Rabbit," I shouted as I ran. I nearly ran into Squirrel coming down the path. "I'm just off to find Rabbit and then Hedgehog is going to tell us his idea." I didn't stay to hear Squirrel's reply as I ran off into the woods looking for Rabbit.

"Hey, Rabbit," I called when I saw him tying a string across the undergrowth between two trees. "What are you doing? Someone could fall over that."

"Oh really, do you think so, well I wouldn't have thought of that."

"Rabbit, you were doing it deliberately weren't you?"

"Who me?" He waved his paw towards his chest in a mock gesture.

"Rabbit!"

"Oh, all right," he said untying the string.

"Hedgehog wants you to come and be part of his idea."

His face brightened. "Really? Me? But… well I'd love to. Ok, where's the party?" And he bounced through the woods leaving me to run to catch up.

When we arrived, Hedgehog cleared his throat in a very

important manner. "I've been thinking about setting up a youth club, for all the young animals to get together and keep out of trouble."

"That's brilliant," Squirrel and I chorused. I was genuinely excited by the idea.

"But I like trouble," Rabbit said.

"I have no idea where we could meet," he continued, "but I want to do something that will help any young animals that, like me, would end up falling in with a bad set and getting into difficulty."

"Like me," Rabbit said proudly, "except I seem to have met all of you."

"That's precisely my point." Hedgehog nodded enthusiastically. "We need to be there for all the young animals such as you, Rabbit, so that they can have fun without getting into trouble."

It wasn't long before we turned our attentions to planning the youth club, and life began to develop a new pattern of 'normal', with us spending most of our daytimes together, although Hedgehog opted out of the longer walks and the rougher games.

"It's always best I don't take part in games where I might accidentally impale someone on my quills," he said very seriously. "It can be a very nasty experience."

I remembered trying to hug Hedgehog and couldn't help but agree with him.

The youth club plans were coming along. Hedgehog wanted it to be for 'any young animal that, according to its species, had not yet achieved adulthood, but which is able to feed and take care of itself'. I was quite relieved about that last bit. I didn't fancy clearing up after any mishaps, or feeding the younger ones. The plan was to hold the meetings on a Tuesday afternoon and evening, in a clearing on the near side of the wood.

The clearing was big enough to provide space for games and seating, but small enough to still be cosy and feel safe for the youngsters. Hedgehog had decided to use some of his savings to help set things up. He assured us that the money had not come from crime, though he wouldn't go as far as to say where it had come from.

Hedgehog also had another plan that was as important as the first one. "I'm going to try to pay back the money that I stole over the years," he announced.

Although it was a brilliant idea, it wasn't going to be that straightforward. "Do you know who you stole everything from?" I asked.

"How are you going to do it?" asked Squirrel. "You can't just go and ring someone's bell and say 'Excuse me I stole your treasured belongings several years ago. I can't give them back to you because I sold them. However, here is the money I got for them. I'm sorry.'"

"Oh, Hedgehog, do tell me about all the crimes you committed," Rabbit said.

Hedgehog frowned at Rabbit. "The important thing is that I'm going to try. It's important to me to make amends in any way I can. I know it won't be easy, but I owe it to all the animals to try."

We were delighted that Hedgehog was so determined to show he really meant what he said about his new life. However, we couldn't help thinking of all the difficulties. Some animals might be less than impressed with how little he had sold their personal possessions for. The first problem was finding out whether they lived at the same addresses. "You could try asking PC Badger to help," I said cautiously.

"I'm sure there may be another way of doing it."

Hedgehog seemed less than keen on involving the Woodland Police.

We worked as hard as we could drawing posters for the youth club and then spent the following day going around the forest sticking them up on trees and notice boards.

"Do you think anyone will come?" asked Squirrel.

"I suppose it will depend on how happy their parents are with the idea," I said. "We will be there, that will be a start."

"I'm coming, I'm coming." Rabbit bounced on the spot as he spoke.

I laughed. "Oh I don't think there will be any shortage of younger ones wanting to see Hedgehog for themselves. He has become a bit of a celebrity."

"Well I hope their parents let them come. Otherwise Hedgehog will be so disappointed." Squirrel sighed.

CHAPTER 14
THE NAMING OF HEDGEHOG

By Saturday, Hedgehog had settled in to his pile of leaves. "I've been thinking."

"Oh?" I wasn't sure if this was a good sign.

"I want a name."

"You've got one. You're called Hedgehog."

Hedgehog laughed. "That's exactly my point. I'm called Hedgehog and I'm a hedgehog. You on the other hand are a dog and you're not called 'Dog'."

I was a little slow in understanding, but began to see what he meant. "I'm called Alfie because that was what the Boss called me."

"Exactly."

"I do use Dog as my surname though. Alfie isn't my real name."

"I'm sorry," said Hedgehog, "what did you just say?"

"I said I use 'Dog' as my surname."

"No the other bit of what you said." He sounded excited.

"Did you mean the bit about Alfie not being my real name?"

"Yes, that bit. Go on."

"Well, it isn't the one my mum gave me. She called me Einstein, probably in the hope that I'd become a great scientist, but the Boss decided that at home I should be called Alfie."

"So at home, I could be called something other than

Hedgehog?" He was jumping up and down as best as a hedgehog can jump.

"Well yes, I suppose so. What would you like to be called?"

"I don't know." He started to calm down. "Perhaps Squirrel could think of something for me."

We went off in search of Squirrel.

"Squirrel, Squirrel," he shouted as we approached the oak tree. "What name shall I have?"

Squirrel poked her head out of the window. "What's all the fuss?" She was looking concerned.

"Hedgehog wants a new name," I said, "and now he needs our help to think of one."

Squirrel immediately understood the problem. It was one she had thought about for herself, so she had no difficulty in seeing why this was something Hedgehog would want. She did a little dance with excitement, something that I had never seen her do before.

"I want one too. Oh, can I have my own name. It would be so good to be known as something that was special just to me and not the same as all the other squirrels. It gets so confusing when we all get together. Oh, Alfie, please think of names for us."

"Oh dear what have I started?" I put my paws over my eyes.

Squirrel suddenly stopped her jig, turned to Hedgehog and said, "You don't think the other animals might be suspicious of you changing your name, given the past, do you?"

Hedgehog gave it some thought. "That's part of the reason I want to do it. I'm a new hedgehog now and I'm going to live a good life."

"So what are we going to be called?" Squirrel asked. We

all sat thinking for a few minutes in silence, but none of us had the least idea.

"We could ask Rabbit," I suggested.

"Oh dear." Hedgehog laughed. "Can you imagine the suggestions he might come up with?"

We decided we should all go away and think about it and see whether we could come up with anything suitable.

By Monday, the preparations for the youth club were keeping us busy. Hedgehog was proud to unveil the purchases he'd had delivered that morning.

"What do you think of this?" He struggled to pull the covers off the table tennis table. "Then there's this." He proudly showed us a little hifi that ran off batteries.

"They're amazing." I picked up one of the table tennis bats. "Although some of the animals might find it a bit difficult to play."

"Nonsense," he said. "I'm sure they can always make up their own rules to get around any bits that are too difficult. After all isn't that what children do all the time?"

"I'm going to set up a little tuck shop," said Squirrel proudly.

"And I've got everything ready for the membership register," I said.

"I'm going to be the DJ. Check this out." Rabbit pulled his sunglasses out and put them on. "I'm like totally buzzing."

We all fell about laughing as Rabbit tried to find the right button to turn the music on.

"This is all well and good." Hedgehog adjusted his glasses. "Everything seems to be ready for the youth club, but what are we going to be called? We still need names."

"How about Dude, dude?" Rabbit said.

"I don't think Dude's a name." I had a good scratch as I

tried to think.

"Well it should be. You could start a fashion, Hedgehog."

Suddenly I stopped scratching. "I've got an idea. We could pick some letters and see what they make. How many letters would you like your names to have?"

"Alfie has five," said Hedgehog. "If it's good enough for you, it should be good enough for me."

"Oh no." Squirrel clasped her paws together. "I think as a girl I should have a long name. It also needs to be in proportion to your surname. Alfie's surname is Dog so he needs a short first name, but both our surnames will be longer so we should have longer first names to go with them."

"We could just all swap," Rabbit said. "Bagsy me Squirrel."

"You don't look much like a Squirrel," I said.

"You don't look much like an Alfie, but I won't hold that against you," Rabbit replied indignantly.

"I didn't think you were changing your name anyway."

"I'm not," Rabbit said, "but that wasn't the point."

"Have you two decided how long you want your names to be?" I asked.

"Yes," said Squirrel and "No," said Hedgehog both at the same time. They continued their discussion on the advantages and disadvantage of long and short names. I must have fallen asleep as Squirrel woke me when she tapped my nose gently.

"We've decided. I want eight letters and Hedgehog wants six."

No sooner had they decided on the number than they started arguing about which letters to use.

The first Woodland Youth Club began on Tuesday

afternoon. Hedgehog, Squirrel, Rabbit and I worked very hard to get everything ready and the clearing in the wood looked perfect. We found some bunting to put up and a few balloons and we were quite prepared for however many animals turned up. Hedgehog was confident that there would be some young animals. Squirrel and I said privately that we were worried that none of the parents would let their youngsters come, in case Hedgehog was a bad influence. We were quite prepared in case Hedgehog was going to be disappointed and decided what the right things would be to say. We also thought it would be best for Squirrel to do the talking if that happened, just to be on the safe side. I was completely ready to stand next to Squirrel whilst she spoke but after the den fiasco, we both thought it might be best if I kept quiet.

We were still in the process of putting the bunting up when I noticed the first pair of eyes watching us through the trees. Then as soon as the cuckoo chimed two you could hear the rustling amongst the leaves and firstly Deer arrived, with one of his sisters and then three of Rabbit's brothers and sisters bounced in. It wasn't long before there were a couple of stoats and a mole as well and they were all having a great time.

Rabbit was having great fun playing the music. "This is MC Rabbit playing the latest tunes. Check this out." He didn't seem at all bothered that they weren't really the latest tunes and that he had to make do with the ones I'd borrowed from home. He simply stood there, chewing a bit of straw, and lifting his dark glasses occasionally so that he could see what was going on.

One of the younger bunnies kept going up to all the other animals and pointing to Rabbit and proudly saying, "That's my brother."

By seven o' clock when it was time to go home everyone was good friends and looking forward to coming back the next week.

Part way through the fun Hedgehog cleared his throat and attracted all the youngsters' attention. "Squirrel and I were wondering if you could possibly help us with finding some names." He then tried to explain about wanting a name to go in front of 'Hedgehog' and that Squirrel felt the same but with 'Squirrel'.

He was still building up to explaining about the letters when one of the bunnies shouted out, "You should be called Harry, Uncle Harry. Uncle Harry Hedgehog." The others picked up on it immediately and before he knew what was happening all the youngsters were calling him Uncle Harry. Hedgehog grinned from ear to ear. "I don't think I can remember any time in my life that I have felt happier than I do right now."

Squirrel was looking very sad and started to move away to a quiet corner. As she did, Deer called out, "And Squirrel should be something really beautiful, because she's so beautiful." A little cheer went up and then the animals made all sorts of suggestions, until one of the older ones shouted, "Nicole".

"Oh," said Squirrel tearfully, "I like that very much. Do you really think I could be a Nicole?" And another little cheer went up from all of them.

As the animals all left to go home, they shouted back, "Goodnight, Uncle Harry. Goodnight, Nicole. Goodnight, Alfie. Goodnight, MC Rabbit."

And we all chorused back, "Goodnight," then collapsed exhausted, but happy, into some of the more comfortable chairs. Once we had recovered a little, we talked about how wonderful it had all been and then raised a glass to celebrate the success of the first session of the Woodland Youth Club.

With the youth club underway Harry Hedgehog could turn his attention to his other plan; the repayment for the things he'd stolen. He explained that he'd thought very carefully and had decided that calling on animals to repay them might be a bad idea. He was starting with a less direct approach.

"I've printed some notices," he explained. "I don't know whether they say the right thing but I did my best."

"Why didn't you tell us you were doing them before?" I asked.

"I really felt this was something I should do on my own. It was me who lived such a bad life and it's me that needs to put it right. I do need your help, but I wanted the poster to be what I had to say. I know I'm not as good with words as you are, Nicole, but I needed to try."

"I'm sorry," I said "I didn't mean to suggest that you were wrong to do it without us, I was just surprised. Can we read what you've put?"

"You can do better than that," said Harry. "You can put them up on all the notice boards around the wood. I'm not tall enough to reach on my own." Then he gave us each a pile of posters.

Rabbit spread one out and read,

"To whom it may concern.

I just wanted to say that I Harry Hedgehog am truly sorry for all the harm I've caused throughout my life. I didn't understand how much my actions would hurt other animals, but I can now understand the pain and heartache that I've caused.

Would any animal who has been the victim of a crime committed by me, please come forward so that I can apologise in person. I will then repay you as best I can.

Yours Harry Hedgehog."

"What do you think?" asked Harry, fidgeting.

"Oh, Harry," said Nicole, "it's lovely. How could anyone not believe that you mean it?"

"I'm really very nervous about it," he said. "I'm worried they might think I want to con them again and so not come forward."

"I think it's really cool," Rabbit said.

"You're being very brave," I said. "Even if it takes a while the animals will realise you mean it sooner or later. You may just need to be patient."

"I've arranged to see the Woodland Bank too," he said.

We gasped.

"Well," he continued, "if I'm going to put things right I can't ignore my role in the theft of money from them and then the money-laundering. I wanted at least to tell them I was sorry and see if I can help them to work out better systems to stop it happening in future."

"Wow," I said, "that does sound very interesting. Do you think I could come with you?"

"I'd like to know all about it too," Rabbit said.

"No," said Harry gently. "This is something I have to do on my own."

CHAPTER 15
HARRY MAKES AMENDS

Nicole, Rabbit and I set off around the wood with the posters and put them up at different levels, to make sure they were easy to see for all heights of animal. When we finished we headed back and saw a queue already starting to form outside Harry's pile of leaves.

"I wonder if he really stole from all of them," Rabbit said, looking wide-eyed.

"I don't know," said Nicole.

"He's one cool hedgehog."

"Rabbit!" Nicole shook her head.

When we went back past Harry's house later, there was still a queue of a magpie, a deer and two weasels. Harry was sitting at a little table just outside his front door. He looked up when he saw us

"It looks as though you're going to be busy for a while," I said. "We wondered if you wanted to come for a picnic?"

"Oh right," he replied wistfully. "I would have liked that." Then shaking his head, he said, "No, thank you, not this time. It's much more important that I finish this. It wouldn't look very good if I left the queue waiting here whilst I went off enjoying myself, maybe next time."

By the time we got back, Harry was still sitting there.

"I'm exhausted," he said. "You know I really don't remember having done some of the things that these animals have told me I'm responsible for. I suppose I must have done. I wasn't a very nice hedgehog really."

"Are you absolutely certain that it was you who did them?" I asked.

"Do you think they would make it up?" asked Harry surprised. "Well I suppose it's a thought. I might have a word with PC Badger at some point, to see if I can get a copy of the list of reported crimes. If I'm going to change how the other animals see me though, I really do need to start by showing them that I believe them and that I'm not trying to get out of what I've said I'll do. And now," he said yawning, "I really need to go for a very long sleep."

When I went to see Harry, the following morning, there was a little notice on his door, 'Sleeping, please call back Monday.'

As I walked away, a weasel came scurrying in my direction. "I've just seen the notice," she said, out of breath. "Is it true?"

"Is what true?" I asked, miles away.

"That Hedgehog is paying people back," puffed the weasel, "for the things he stole?"

"Oh yes. Did he steal from you too?"

"No, no. It's just that there's a lovely elderly mole who lives quite near me and I know he stole a ring from her. It would mean so much to her if she could get it back."

"I don't think that Harry, that is Hedgehog, has any of the things he stole anymore," I said, trying not to disappoint the weasel.

"But maybe he knows where it went?" said the weasel almost pleading me to do something. "Maybe there is some way to get it back?"

"I suppose there might be," I said. "I don't really know how you get rid of stolen things. I don't suppose you eat a ring."

"No, I don't suppose you do," said Weasel shaking her

head. "Well I'd better go to see him."

"He's asleep today," I said, trying to be helpful.

"Well why didn't you say so?" asked the weasel. "I could have done something useful with all this time we've been standing here talking. When is he going to wake up?"

"Tomorrow, I think."

"Very well, I shall just have to come back tomorrow." And with that she bustled away.

All weekend the rain came down. I wasn't sure it was safe to sleep in a pile of leaves in such awful weather. There were puddles forming everywhere, but Harry's leaves were in a sheltered spot and remained reasonably dry.

By the time I did see him on Monday, he had put together a list of forty-two animals who he'd stolen from.

"I suppose," he said, "that means somewhere close to half of the thefts I committed have been accounted for. I didn't keep an exact count of the things I did, but I've got a fair idea."

"Did Weasel find you?" I asked.

"Weasel?" said Harry and just as he did so, Weasel scurried up to us to have Mole added to the list.

"So that's forty-three," said Harry when she'd gone. "I'm planning to visit each of them individually over the next few weeks to give them chance to discuss with me the impact that the theft had and for me to see how I can make amends. More animals may come forward, when they get to see the notice, but I've got plenty to be going on with. Some of the animals may have moved away and it may take them a while to hear what I'm doing. Later today, I thought I'd better see the mice that went to the length of trying to pretend they were a relative. One of the deer has agreed to give me a lift. It isn't going to be an easy journey and it'll be dangerous in places. The deer is planning to use it as an opportunity to see his cousin at the same time."

"Right," I said, disappointed to be left out. "Good luck. I suppose I shall see you tomorrow."

"You could always come with us," said Harry.

I brightened immediately. "If you're sure I wouldn't be in the way. I'd love to come."

The deer said we would be better to wait until dusk before setting off. The roads would be quieter and there would be fewer people about.

It was strange picking our way through the wood in the half-light. Every twig seemed to crackle more loudly when it was trodden on and I was much more conscious of the sound of the wind blowing through the leaves. I heard rustling behind me and stopped to listen. The rustling seemed to stop and listen too. Then I walked on a step or two and it rustled. As I turned around, I was sure I could see a nose sticking out from behind a bush. "Deer, Harry, I think we're being followed."

"Now don't be silly, Alfie, there's no one else with us," Deer said without turning around.

Then the rustle chuckled.

"Rabbit, is that you?" I asked, hesitating.

"Oh bother. You've caught me. I've been following you all the way across the wood. I wanted to see where you were going."

"Now you run along home, Rabbit," Hedgehog said. "Your mother will wonder where you are."

"She always wonders where I am. It'll be fine."

"Rabbit!"

"If you don't let me come, I shall just follow you anyway."

"Deer, what do you think?" Harry asked.

"You'll have to do exactly as I tell you," Deer said.

Rabbit nodded and raised his paw. Grinning he said, "Cross my heart."

Deer nodded. "Let's get moving."

I was just starting to wish I'd stayed at home when we reached a road with street lamps.

"Can we walk along the pavement?" I asked nervously.

"What, and be seen? Good heavens no," replied Deer. "Do you have any idea what would happen around here if a human saw a deer carrying a hedgehog on his back, just walking along the pavement? We'd never hear the last of it. It's all well and good for you, you're a domestic animal, people expect to see you. If they see you walk along a pavement they just think you're well trained. It's never the same for us woodland creatures."

"It's just that I'm not feeling awfully brave," I said, "but I can see what you're saying. I didn't mean to cause trouble."

Deer spoke in a more gentle voice. "You'll be quite safe young puppy, just as long as you stay close by me. Now come along and we'll be there in no time."

"Rabbit, do you think you could stop prodding me too?" I said.

"I'm cool," Rabbit replied.

It didn't take us much longer to reach the place where the mice lived and as word had already been sent ahead of us, they were there waiting for us as planned. Whilst the mice sat down and explained to Harry how upset they were about the things they had lost, I sat and listened quietly learning more about the life Harry had lived before I knew him. When they'd finished he shook the paw of each of the mice in turn and promised he would do his best to put it right.

Then Harry asked Rabbit and me if we would stay with

the mice whilst he went to have a word with the deer.

"Show us how you did it?" Rabbit said as soon as Harry had gone.

The mice ran around collecting an overcoat and the other props they'd used and then one climbed on the shoulders of the other and they wrapped the coat around them to hide their bodies.

"I've got to have a photo," Rabbit said, clapping his paws together in delight. "Who's got a camera?"

It wasn't long before one of the mice had found a camera and taken Rabbit's picture standing with his arm around the pretend hedgehog. The mouse scurried off to print it out so that we would have it in time for Harry coming back.

It was quite late by the time we all waved our goodbyes to the mice and set off for home. I had hoped we would wait until daylight, but Deer said that was too risky. I found it hard to believe that moving by day could be any more risky than it felt right now. I stayed as close as I could, with Rabbit in front of me so that I could see what he was doing. Sometimes I was so close that I trod on Deer's hoof. Deer was starting to get a little annoyed, particularly as he was already having to deal with being prickled by Harry's quills every so often, but we managed to get back without Deer once shouting at either of us.

CHAPTER 16
HEDGEHOG'S STORY

I needn't have worried about the youth club. Not only did all the previous week's animals turn up, but a few new ones as well. There were a whole family of bunnies that I hadn't met before. Their mum had decided it was a good idea to get them out of the way to give her a better chance of doing all the mopping up from the rain. Their Family burrow had completely flooded and they all had to stay with their aunt until it dried out again.

It was lovely hearing all the young animals calling Hedgehog 'Uncle Harry'. Half way through the afternoon, Harry got everyone together and said he wanted to tell them all a story. The animals gathered around and he began in the traditional fashion.

"Once upon a time there was a family of deer living just near here. There was a mummy and a daddy deer and one little fawn. Now the little fawn had not been very strong when he was born and his parents didn't know whether he would live or not. Anyway, the mummy and daddy deer did everything they could to take care of their little fawn through the summer and then in the autumn he became quite poorly. All through the winter, they nursed him. He was their only fawn and they loved him very much. As spring approached, he started to get stronger and as his first birthday came around it looked as though he was going to be strong enough to make it after all. His mummy and daddy were so delighted that he was going to be all right that they wanted to do something very special for his first birthday, to be able to celebrate the fact that they hadn't lost him. The little fawn's parents didn't have very much money, but they wanted everything to be perfect for their little one. They gathered all his favourite foods to have a little family party. When his birthday arrived Mummy and Daddy deer went to the pantry to get everything out as a surprise for their little fawn, but what do you think? It had all gone. Someone had stolen the food they had put away specially."

At this point, the animals listening to Harry all gasped in horror. Harry gave them plenty of time to take in what had happened. There were youngsters shouting out "What happened next, Uncle Harry?" "Finish the story."

When Harry started again, he spoke with some difficulty. "I was the one who had taken the food." There were more gasps from the crowd of young animals. Then Harry continued, "I was living on the streets back then. I didn't have a home of my own, or anyone to look after me. I didn't realise how much upset I would cause by taking the food. I had no idea just how important that day had been to the deer. Well, I have now talked to the deer's family. They said to me that if only I had told them I was in need, they would willingly have shared some of the food with me and that I really hadn't needed to resort to stealing. Even though they had so little, they would have shared it rather than see an animal go hungry." Harry was quiet for a moment, none of the youngsters spoke. They sat enthralled waiting for what Harry was going to say next. "What I'm trying to tell you," he began slowly, "is that it is never right just to take things that don't belong to you and even if at the time you think you've got a reason and it doesn't seem very bad, you just don't know how important it was to the person you're taking from. Stealing is never the right thing to do." Then he went on to say how sorry he had been when he found out how much sadness he had caused in the deer household that night. The animals stayed sitting quietly in front of Harry, while Nicole and I stood at the back.

When Harry finished talking, one of the deer at the back moved forward and hugged him and said, "Uncle Harry, it was my dad's birthday. He was the fawn that was going to be given the party. Well I just wanted you to know that he forgives you and we'd love it if you would come around and have tea with us tomorrow."

Then all the other animals cheered and Nicole had tears in her eyes.

By the end of Youth Club, none of the animals wanted to go home. All the young animals reluctantly went on their way and were already talking about how much they were looking forward to next week.

It was a couple of days before it finally stopped raining for long enough to see my friends again. I didn't much like the rain. It was always so difficult getting my coat clean again after I'd been out in the mud. When I eventually ventured out, I bumped into Rabbit.

"About time somebody showed up," he said. "There must be something fun we could be doing. How about knocking on old Mr Woodpecker's door and running away."

"I don't think we should. Let's go and see if Hedgehog's doing anything."

Nicole arrived just after us.

Harry poured out some lemonade and then as we sat there, he started telling us about another visit to a victim of one of his crimes.

"Many of the animals who have come forward don't want any compensation," said Harry. "They've already received money from their insurers. One or two have said that it's good enough for them that I'm really sorry and trying to make amends. In fact some of the animals have suggested that I should use the money to either improve the youth club or to set up a little scholarship fund. The fund could make sure that orphaned animals get the same opportunities in life that the other young animals do."

"That's a lovely idea," I said.

Harry continued, "Anyway, I did visit the elderly mole that Weasel came to tell me about. She said that the ring I took had been her grandmother's and it was her most treasured possession. She would do anything to have it back and make sure that she could pass it to her daughter and keep it in the family. I've been desperately trying to remember what I did with it when I stole it. Unfortunately, it's quite a long time ago and whilst the mole can remember exactly when it was and how it all happened, I'm struggling to remember what I did afterwards. It really shows me how the things I did scarred the victims." He looked away sadly.

"How did you usually sell things?" Rabbit asked.

"I used a number of different contacts, depending on what it was. There were a couple of antique dealers and jewellers that would buy things from me for cash and then there were some middle animals that I could go through if I needed to get the item out of the area. There's nothing else for it, I'm going to have to look up some of my old underworld contacts and see if any of them can help."

"That is so cool," Rabbit said. "Can I come with you?"

"What would your mother say?" Harry said, smiling at Rabbit.

"Oh dear," I said. "Do you really think that's such a good idea? I mean, what if any of them try to entice you back into a life of crime?"

"Alfie!" said Nicole sternly. "Have you no faith in Harry at all?" She moved a little closer to him. "I believe in you."

I felt strangely uncomfortable, which was not helped when Harry winked at me.

"Yes of course I have faith in Harry," I snapped. "It was just…"

Before I could go any further, Harry said, "I'll be just fine and besides I might actually get you to help. I need a couple of days to do some work first, but it might just be that I will have something you can all help with if you'd like to."

Both Rabbit and I agreed without thinking to ask what we'd have to do.

"I'll see you back here the day after tomorrow," said Harry. "Now if you'll excuse me there are some people I need to make contact with."

I was still worried about Harry, for all Nicole had said. It wasn't that I didn't trust him, it was just that I realised how tempting it might be. It would be much better if Harry had nothing to do with his previous life. I left Rabbit and Nicole and went to sit by the stream. I watched it going by, until being mesmerised by the water I fell asleep.

I woke up as a little boat was drifting by and a gruff voice called across to the bank, "Hey you."

"Who me?" I looked round to see if there was anyone behind me.

"Yes," said the voice that was coming from a rather large dog, with a very serious look about him. "I'm looking for Hedgehog. Where can I find him?" There was no please, just a brusque question, barked out.

I felt protective of my friend. "It depends who's looking for him?" I sounded rather braver than I was feeling.

"The Rat," said the dog, which confused me. "I heard he was out of prison and he's looking for me."

"Oh," I said, not knowing what to say next. On the one paw if Harry was looking for 'The Rat' it seemed wrong not to tell him the way, but on the other paw, I really didn't like the look of this fellow and I wasn't sure that Harry seeing him would be such a good idea. "Look, if you moor your boat over there under the trees, I'll find Harry and get him to come here."

"Harry?" said The Rat.

"Yes, Harry Hedgehog. He used to be known as just Hedgehog." Then I ran off, before The Rat had time to tie the boat up and follow me. I arrived at Harry's house just in time to hear paws behind me and found that The Rat had caught me up rather sooner than I expected.

I was puffing a bit and was just trying to point with my paw when The Rat came into sight.

"Hedgehog," shouted The Rat, with genuine warmth. "How are you?"

"Rat!" exclaimed Harry raising a paw to high five in greeting.

"Right then," I said. "I'll leave you two to it," and I sloped off towards the river.

I was now seriously worried about Harry making contact with his underworld connections. I was quite sure if Nicole had seen 'The Rat' she would have understood my concern. I didn't want to see Harry give up on all the good things that were happening, but then I thought that the fact that Harry was giving all his money away, ought to show that it's not material things that mattered to him anymore.

CHAPTER 17
THE RAT

When I met up with Harry a couple of days later, I started to realise just how sheltered my puppyhood had been. Harry had spent the last couple of days tracking down 'The Rat' 'The Mole' and 'The Snake' and as with The Rat, those were just their nicknames rather than their species. He was doing all of this just to track down the ring for Mole.

"Well," said Harry, "it's fortunate that the ring is a little out of the ordinary, otherwise after all this time there would be no hope that any of my contacts would remember it. He chuckled. "It turns out that it's 'The Mole' who recalls the ring and thinks he sold it to a dealer in the City. Fortunately, he is still in contact with the dealer and says for a price he'll make some enquiries."

"That's great," I said cautiously. "Where do we come in?"

"Well." Harry scratched his nose. "I was wondering if we could make the trip ourselves. I don't want any money passing between me and my old criminal friends for any services. I really don't want to find myself in the position of any favours being done that could be called in later. I know you're worried about me Alfie, but I really do want to stay on the straight and narrow and I have a good idea of how things like this can go wrong."

I was very relieved to hear him say so. I was about to start questioning the practicality of heading all the way to the City, when I was taken aback to find a bright cheerful

Nicole come bustling out of Harry's house with a small broom.

"I, er, I was just helping Harry." She looked embarrassed.

"Oh," I said, feeling a sudden pang. I thought back to the time when Nicole had been just my friend and how fond of her I was. Harry started talking to me again and I had to pull myself back to listening.

"Harry, how do you think we will be able to make such a long journey, crossing so many busy roads and do it safely? You were worn out just walking back from the far wood. I just can't see that it's possible."

Harry started to fidget with some papers. "I thought that perhaps. Well that is to say. I was wondering."

"What Harry is trying to say," said Nicole, softly laying her paw on his arm, "was, do you think that it would be possible for The Boss to give us all a lift into the City in the car?"

"Yes." Harry looked relieved. "That was exactly what I was trying to say. Do you Alfie?"

"Well!" I sat down in surprise. "The Boss knows you're all my friends, but I haven't told her about some of the things we're doing and I certainly haven't told her about the things you used to do, Harry. I thought it might be best to keep her out of it, just in case she didn't understand. Are you really suggesting that a hedgehog, a squirrel, a rabbit and a dog should get a lift into the middle of the City?"

"I suppose we don't all have to go," said Harry. "It's probably too dangerous for Nicole to go anyway."

"It's for a good cause, Alfie. Just think how happy we could make an elderly mole."

"Yes I know," I said sadly, "but it does seem rather impossible. I can't see how we could take Harry either, he'd never be able to climb in. I see what you mean about not wanting to pay 'The Mole' to go, especially if he's going to want a favour in return. It would be awful to find yourself involved in illegal activities again and I can't imagine the required favour would be something legal. I suspect that the dealer would be much happier to help Nicole than to help me. I do see the point about her safety though and I wouldn't want anything to happen to her. I don't suppose there's anything else for it. I shall just have to go with Rabbit; although, it still depends on whether I can get The Boss to take us."

"Oh, Alfie do you really think..." said Harry.

"You're so brave, Alfie," said Nicole, and my heart melted.

"Oh it's nothing," I said shyly. "I'll talk to The Boss now, if I can find her."

I trotted off in the direction of the house, talking to myself as I went. "Do you think you could give me a lift? Would it be possible to go into the City? Can I borrow the car?" No that last one clearly wasn't going to work. Oh dear, what had I got myself into?

When I arrived back at the house, I found The Boss at work in the office.

"Hmmm." I cleared my throat, but got no reaction. In these situations, I always feel it's inappropriate to launch straight into something, so I tried a different approach.

"Woof." Then again, "Woof, woof."

The Boss looked up from her work and smiled at me. She never failed to make time for me when I really wanted it. Fortunately, I was still just about small enough to climb onto her knee and from there I could persuade her more easily. I put my front paws up onto her knee and allowed her to lift me up. Then I snuggled as closely as I could. Once

I'd allowed her to give my tummy a good rub, I licked her and then cleared my throat again.

"Hmm." It was always difficult to know where to start in a conversation with a human. "I was wondering, would it be possible for us to go into the City together?" I didn't think it was wise to ask for a lift for Rabbit too, he'd just have to hide under my blanket again. It would be easier with only him to get in, rather than Squirrel as well.

I was really looking for a simple yes or no as an answer. In truth, I wanted a 'no', so that I didn't have to go through with it. What I hadn't anticipated was being asked questions.

"Why do you want to go to the City? It's so busy and dirty. There aren't very many trees and green spaces. Why don't we go to the park instead?"

This wasn't going well. Any other day I would have jumped at the chance of going to the park. "No, I really need to go to the City. Please can we go there?" I wished that she would just accept that was what I needed.

"But why do you need to go there?"

"It's a long story."

"I'm listening," she said, scratching me behind the ear.

Trying to explain to someone that your friend is a criminal, is not a good starting point. Trying to explain that you want to go, on their behalf, to talk to someone that was in receipt of some of those stolen goods, does not look good. By the time I'd finished I had to explain all about Harry, his life of crime and how he was now trying to put things right. I also explained about the elderly mole and the ring.

Eventually the questions stopped and she looked at me thoughtfully, "I would rather that you weren't mixed up in all this. But given that you are and that you're doing it for the right reasons, I will take you."

I was delighted and just a little relieved. I jumped up and down on The Boss's knee and gave her the biggest lick a dog can give. "Thank you," I woofed. "I'd better tell Harry."

"We'll go on Thursday," said The Boss as I jumped down and trotted off towards the garden.

When I found Harry and Nicole, they were on their way out with all sorts of bits and pieces piled up.

"We're going to decorate the Youth Club," Harry announced.

"Oh right, can I help?"

"Of course you can," said Nicole. "We were going to wait for you, but we didn't know how long you'd be. How did you get on?"

We met Rabbit on the way and as we walked towards the Youth Club's area of the wood, I told them all about having to tell The Boss the whole story and how she had eventually agreed to the plan.

"Couldn't I sit in the front seat this time?" Rabbit asked putting his head on one side in a pleading expression.

"No, Rabbit. Either you stowaway or you don't come."

"Life just ain't fair. I guess I'll go with the first option."

"That's marvellous," said Harry, tripping over the paper he was carrying in his excitement. "Absolutely marvellous," he repeated as he bent down to start piling everything up again. The glue had rolled away under a bush and I fished it out with my paw.

"How exactly are we going to decorate an outdoor space?" I asked. "I thought decorating was an indoor type of thing."

"Well we were going to just tidy it up a bit and then maybe hang some decorations in the trees," said Nicole.

"Right."

When we arrived, the first job was to sweep away the layer of leaves, but even that proved to be difficult. No sooner had Rabbit carefully brushed the leaves into a little pile in the corner, than the wind blew them all back to the places they started from. "This is a great game," he shouted. "Why don't you try, Alfie."

"Maybe if we build a roof to shelter the area it would be better," said Harry eagerly.

"Won't we need planning permission for that?" I asked.

"I don't think so," said Harry, "not just to put up a bit of shelter. Can you find me some sticks Alfie? And try not to chew them on the way back."

It would have been a funny sight, if any of the other animals had been there to see us, me running back and forth collecting twigs and branches, then Nicole running up the trees to tie them into position. Harry stood and directed proceedings from the ground, while Rabbit lay back against a tree watching. It was slow going and we didn't manage to complete very much, but it was a start and was enough to keep any rain off the table tennis.

Putting the decorations up proved a little easier than building the shelter. Harry sat and cut out shapes and threaded them onto strings that Nicole was able to hang from tree branches. It wasn't much but it made the place look brighter now that the blossom had gone from the trees. By the time we'd finished, we were very tired and needed a rest. We agreed to meet to finish things off the following afternoon before Youth Club began.

CHAPTER 18
AN ARGUMENT

The afternoon following putting up the decorations, the sound of happy young voices echoed through the trees. At least they did until one of the deer got into an argument with his cousin. It was all very silly really. The older deer had borrowed the younger one's MP3 player and then lost it, so he wasn't able to give it back when the younger one wanted it. The older one had been trying to avoid seeing the younger one, but had so wanted to come to youth club that he took the risk that his cousin would be there.

As soon as he realised there was trouble taking off, Harry got hold of both of the deer and led them to the back of the Youth Club to sit down. "So what's this all about?" he asked in a gentle fatherly manner.

"He's lost my MP3 player," wailed the younger deer.

"I really didn't mean to," said the older one. "One minute I'd got it and the next I hadn't. I just don't know where it went. I must have dropped it in the forest, but it could be anywhere. I spent ages trying to look for it, but I couldn't see it."

"I wouldn't have lent it to you if I thought you weren't going to look after it," said the younger one. "It was a present from my mum. She had to save up for ages to buy it for me."

The older deer looked down at the ground. "I didn't realise. I'm sorry. I didn't mean to lose it. I don't know what I can do."

"I know you wouldn't do it deliberately," said the younger one, looking up for the first time. "It was just special to me."

"How would it be," intervened Harry talking to the older deer, "if you could earn some money to buy a replacement?"

"Oh yes," he said, "but where can I earn that much money?"

"Well," said Harry "what if you were to do the cleaning up after Youth Club every week for the next ten weeks and I were to pay you for doing it?"

"Would you really?" said the older deer.

"Yes," said Harry and turning to the younger one he asked, "would that be acceptable to you?"

"Oh, Uncle Harry, thank you," he said. "That would be so good."

The two cousins went off happily together for a game of darts. I tried my paw at table tennis. I held the bat in my mouth to play, I found it easier than using my paws and was doing quite well, until in my excitement I bit too hard and got my tooth stuck in the wood of the bat. It took two of the rabbits to pull the bat off again. After that, I stuck to watching and listening to the music that MC Rabbit was playing.

When it came to time to go home, as the other animals waved their goodbyes, without being reminded, the older deer went to fetch the broom and started to do all the tidying up. Harry stayed behind with him, to keep him company while the rest of us headed for home, tired but happy from another successful evening.

The following day, I was enjoying a lazy morning after the hectic couple of days that had started the week. I managed to persuade myself to get out of bed, but only so that I could move outside to the shade then go back to sleep. I was in the middle of a lovely dream when I was rudely awoken by a prod from Harry.

"Alfie, wake up, read this." He thrust an envelope in my direction as I sat rubbing my eyes.

"Hello, Harry, did you want something." I yawned.

He pushed the letter at me again. "Read this."

"What is it?" I asked.

"I don't know," he said. Which didn't seem a very helpful answer.

I took the letter from Harry and removed it from the envelope:

"Dear Mr Hedgehog,

Re: The Woodland Youth Club

The Woodland Council would be grateful if you could attend their meeting at 7.30pm on 9th June, to be held at the Council Chamber, Middle of the Wood, at which we would like to discuss the matter of The Woodland Youth Club.

Yours sincerely
The Woodland Council"

"Oh I see." I scratched my head with my back paw. "What do you think they want?"

"I was rather hoping you might have some idea. I really don't know," he said wringing his little brown paws.

"I'm sure it will be fine." I yawned again, got up, did a little circle to get comfortable and prepared to lie down to continue my dream. "We haven't done anything wrong, and all the animals enjoy it and their parents keep letting them come back."

"I don't know," he said, "with my background, I wouldn't blame them for not wanting me to do it, but it seemed such a good idea. It's just over a week until the meeting, you don't suppose I should get a petition started or something do you?" He stopped and gasped. "You don't think it's because of the deer fighting do you?"

I sat up, realising I wasn't going to get chance to finish my nap. "No, I'm sure it isn't that, The Woodland Council would never be able to act that quickly. Besides, you did a great job of sorting that out. What does Nicole think?"

"I didn't want to tell her," he said looking down. "I didn't want her worrying."

"Look, it doesn't say that you can't hold the Youth Club next week does it?"

Harry shook his head.

"And it doesn't mention anything wrong," I continued. "So I think you should stop worrying and I think we should include Nicole, she's been part of this from the start." Harry nodded meekly and then followed me down the path to find her.

Nicole did all she could to cheer Harry up and put a brave face on things. "I don't think we'll be able to come with you," she said, "but Alfie and I will wait at the edge of the wood until you come out. As long as Alfie promises not to chase his tail and pace up and down all the time." She smiled at me.

I grinned back sheepishly.

"You'll be able to tell us everything that happens straight after the meeting."

"It's turning into a bit of a week," I said. "I really must get ready for going into the City tomorrow. I need to work out where I have to go and what to say. I'm not sure it's the sort of thing I'm very good at, I usually end up blurting the wrong thing out in delicate situations. I'll leave you to it. See you later." Waving a paw, I left Nicole to cheer Harry up and headed home.

I started to think seriously about my trip to see the dealer in the City the following day. I thought carefully about my little speech and began rehearsing it in my head. Well mostly in my head, occasionally I forgot I was only practising and started to say it out loud. It wasn't too bad except when the odd passing bird or animal overheard and gave me a funny look.

I didn't like cities much. There were too many pavements and cars and not enough trees and grass. The Boss didn't like them either, for much the same reasons. Rabbit on the other paw was excited as he'd never been to a city and didn't know what to expect.

"Will I be able to look out of the window?"

"No, Rabbit. The Boss won't know you're there. You have to stay under the blanket."

"Not even a little look?"

"Rabbit!"

"No, ok."

We got Rabbit into the car without a hitch and set off. Half way through the journey he poked his head out and whispered, "It's hot in here."

I moved the blanket back over him as quickly as I could. I could feel him wriggling and hoped the Boss didn't turn around and notice.

This city was very busy and noisy. It seemed as though someone was digging up all the roads at the same time and there were the sounds of drills and the smell of dust everywhere. I wanted to get the visit over as quickly as I could.

"If you could just pull up here," I said, "I'll jump out

and see the dealer. You could drive round the block and pick me up in the same spot in five minutes."

"I'm coming with you," said the Boss. "I need to park the car first."

"You can't come," I was horrified. I didn't want her hearing my little speech and how was I going to take Rabbit in.

"I'm sorry, Alfie, I'm not letting you go off into the City on your own. It isn't safe. I can park near here, we won't have far to walk."

It wasn't the walking that bothered me, but there was no point saying anything. I knew when I was beaten. Secretly I think The Boss didn't want to miss out on the excitement, but she wouldn't admit to that. I managed to get Rabbit out and he hid under the car until we started walking. As we went, I turned to see him taking exaggerated steps following behind. When he saw me looking, he hid behind a lamppost, but with his ears sticking out there was no missing where he was.

We eventually found the shop, which had all sorts of things in the window. Everything on display had, previously belonged to someone else. It was one of those times when no matter how often you've rehearsed what you're going to say, it's still not easy when you come to it. I asked The Boss if she would mind waiting by the door, I really didn't want to have to discuss Harry's business in front of her. Then I moved further into the shop and waited for my turn. As I stood there, the shop bell rang and Rabbit came in wearing dark glasses and a hat pulled well down over his face and he leaned up against the counter just behind me.

When it was my turn, I said, "I'm Alfie, I think you've had a call from The Mole about…"

I was in full flow and was suddenly interrupted by the dealer. "I think you should come this way," he said, ushering me through a curtain into a back room. As we went through he said, "These things are really much better discussed in private, don't you think."

I decided he was probably right and I would be much happier if The Boss couldn't watch me. The room behind the shop was absolutely full of boxes and bags all piled up on shelves, or sitting in the middle of the floor and come to that on the chairs as well. It was hard to find a clear bit of floor to sit on, but the dealer made some room for me and cleared a chair for himself. No sooner had I sat down than Rabbit poked his head round the curtain grinning.

The dealer got up quickly. "What…"

"It's ok," I said, "he's with me." The dealer nodded and Rabbit sat down.

I began again. "It was about the ring, it was a very small and quite distinctive one. Harry, that is Hedgehog, sold it to you quite a long time ago. It would have fitted a very small finger and was set with lots of tiny diamonds."

"Oh, I remember it," said the dealer peering over his glasses. "I was able to sell it for quite a lot of money. It was a very beautiful piece and really quite different. Now let me see." The dealer moved across to a table and began to rummage through a large pile of papers, until he came to a big book in which he wrote down all the things he sold. "Yes," he said. "Here it is. I sold it to a very wealthy lady who wanted it as a present for her small daughter, for her dolls house family."

"You don't still have it?" I asked sadly.

"Good heavens no. If I kept things for that length of time I'd never make any money." The dealer laughed.

"Well that's that," Rabbit said, jumping up. "Come on,

Alfie, old chap. We've tried. While we're here, do you think you could just show us some of the things you've got that have been stolen?"

"Rabbit!"

"As far as I know, young man," the dealer said, looking over his spectacles, "nothing that I have here has been stolen."

"No, of course," I said quickly. "Rabbit, would you wait outside please?" Rabbit looked all around him and then slipped out through the curtain keeping his back against the wall.

"I'm really sorry, Sir," I said. "Thank you for your time."

"Just one minute," said the dealer and he scribbled on a piece of paper and handed it to me. "This is where the little girl lives, if it's any use to you. I shouldn't really give it to you, but you seem like a nice puppy and I probably owe Hedgehog a favour or two."

"Oh, he doesn't want any favours," I said quickly. "He is determined to go straight this time."

"And I wish him all the luck in the world," said the dealer laughing again. "He was never a really bad hedgehog, he just did what he had to in order to get by. Now you take this, young Alfie and good luck sorting it out."

"Thank you. I'll do my best." I padded out to the front of the shop, where Rabbit was peering at a display cabinet and The Boss was still waiting patiently.

We managed to get all of us safely back into the car. I didn't say much on the way home. I was wondering if there were any way of going to see the little girl and explaining to her. The problem was that she lived a long way from the wood too, I would have to look at a map to see where it was. If I could get there then at least there was a possibility that she might help. Small children are so much more understanding of these things than adults.

CHAPTER 19
THE WOODLAND BANK

Rabbit and I went to find Harry and Nicole to tell them about our journey into the City. There was no answer at Harry's house so we went straight round to see Nicole.

"He's gone to see the Woodland Bank this morning," she said, proudly. "You should have seen him in his suit, he looked amazing."

"Suit! I'd forgotten about that, with everything else going on."

"It shouldn't be that long until he gets back. We could have a picnic and you can all tell me how you got on."

"That's a great idea. I'll nip home and get some food together and meet you back here." It was always a lovely idea to have a picnic, somehow food always tasted so much better when eaten outdoors.

I struggled to lift the hamper. This was always the hard part. The journey home was so much easier, at least from the hamper's point of view. I got back to Nicole's house as Harry was walking back from his meeting. I couldn't believe the sight of him. There he was, all dressed up, with his hair neatly combed and not an out of place prickly bit in sight. I didn't know what to say. I stood there with my mouth opening and closing and absolutely no sounds coming out.

"What do you think?" said Harry, giving a little twirl.

"Way to go, dude," said Rabbit who was lying propped up, chewing a piece of grass.

"Doesn't he look dapper?" said Nicole, blushing slightly.

"I would never have imagined. Do you think I would look that good in a suit?"

They all laughed.

"Nicole can you put the kettle on while I change?" asked Harry. "I really need to put on something more comfortable. It may look all right, but hedgehogs weren't really designed to wear suits. I don't think you were really designed for a suit either, Alfie."

"I don't suppose suits were designed to be worn by hedgehogs!" I said. "Anyway, we're all going for a picnic. I've got it all here."

"Ok. I'm on my way," he said, scurrying off to his house to change.

Harry said nothing about his meeting whilst we sat and had a cup of tea. He just sat and grinned. Although we were eager for his news, we knew better than to push him. He would tell us in his own good time and until then there was no amount of persuasion that would change his mind.

"Right," said Harry, "your trip was yesterday, so you should go first in telling what happened."

"Oh, it was amazing. We were awesome," said Rabbit before I had any chance to open my mouth. "You should have seen the shop. They had like so much jewellery. Bling city."

Once I could get a word in. I told them about the back room and about all the boxes and eventually I told them about the ledger and the little girl that the ring had gone to, for her dolls' house collection. "So we're no nearer to getting the ring back than we were," I finished.

"No nearer," said Harry, jumping up. "My dear boy, of course we're nearer. This is fantastic. We now know where the ring went. That may mean we know where the ring still is. Don't you see? We may be able to get the ring back."

Harry's enthusiasm was infectious. Nicole began to get very excited at the thought of returning the ring to mole. Only I seemed to be reluctant to enter into the celebrations.

"How are we going to get to the girl?" I asked.

"We'll find a way," Harry said. "We always find a way. Have you looked at the map?"

"Not yet. I haven't really had time."

"Well there you are then," he said.

I wasn't quite sure where that meant we were, but I thought better than asking. I simply said, "I'll look when I get home."

"Very good," said Harry. "Then we can all go to see her and get it sorted."

"But she may not want to sell it to us." I was still struggling to see that it was going to be quite as easy as Harry thought.

"She will," he said confidently. "Little girls always like a story with a happy ending. You'll see."

To be fair I didn't yet know very much about little girls. I could see that a happy ending might be good, but I wasn't sure it would be enough for the girl to part with a treasured possession. Nicole didn't seem to doubt what Harry said, so maybe he was right.

"Right," said Harry, "now it's my turn. I am very excited about going for a picnic, but do you think it could wait for just a little while?"

"Could I munch on a carrot while we're waiting?" asked Rabbit.

Harry smiled at Rabbit. "Just be a little bit patient, we have a visit to make first. Ok then, follow me."

He led us along a path into the nearest bit of wood and

right up to the door of a branch of the Woodland Bank.

"They should be expecting us," he said and rang the bell.

We just looked at each other. A bespectacled hare opened the door and led us all into a small room off the main trunk of the tree.

"I will just need the three of you to sign, here and here," the hare said addressing Nicole, Rabbit and me.

"Why? What are we signing?"

The hare seemed flustered and said that perhaps he would just give us five minutes to ourselves. We looked at Harry.

He looked sheepish. "Well," he explained, "the Woodland Bank has never been offered money back before. They were quite overwhelmed by my wanting to make amends. When I talked to them earlier, the manager said that they would like half of the money to be set aside in something called a 'trust fund' to help orphaned animals in this wood and the surrounding woods. The money is to be used to help them with whatever they need, to make sure that they don't have to turn to crime. As for your signatures, well, they wanted all of us to be the trustees together with the hare that brought us in here. Trustees are people who look after the money and make sure it is all spent correctly."

Nicole had tears streaming down her cheeks and could only nod her agreement. I found just enough space to run around in circles to express my excitement, while Rabbit bounced in between all of us.

The hare came back and looked over his half glasses. "Are we all quite ready now?"

"Yes," said Nicole with a smile that beamed across her face. "We are quite ready."

Once all the paperwork was complete, the hare shook our paws and showed us back towards the main entrance.

"Now can we go and have our picnic?" I asked as we came back out into the daylight.

"Yes," said Harry, "let's celebrate."

I spent the following morning looking at the maps. I was trying to work out where the little girl lived. I had the address that the dealer gave me, but I wasn't absolutely sure how to look it up. I went to find The Boss.

"How do I look something up on a map?"

"Why? What do you need to find?"

There they were again, all those questions, always more questions. As vague as I might try to be, I knew there would be more questions, it was much easier to start with the whole story and besides, I might as well explain everything as I was going to need The Boss's help again if we were going to get to the little girl's house. I sat myself down on a space on the floor, put my head on one paw and began, "I'm still trying to find the ring."

"Which ring?"

"The mole's ring," I said impatiently.

"Oh right. Bring the map here and I'll show you."

I picked the map up and went over to her desk. "This is the address." I laid out the piece of paper. "I've got as far as a bit in the back of the map that says 62 G 3, but I don't know what to do now."

The Boss took the map from me and opened it at page 62.

I was trying to stand on my hind legs and look over The Boss's shoulder, when she made me jump by saying, "Oh look, it's by the park we go to."

It was by the park, which was brilliant news. That would make it easy to see the little girl. My tail was wagging madly. Maybe Harry was right, maybe we were nearer to getting Mole's ring back.

It was Sunday when I next went to find my friends. Harry was sitting at his desk with the list of 'previous crimes' laid out in front of him.

"It's going to take us forever," he said in despair. "I spent so long tracking down my connections for Mole's ring that I have quite overlooked some of these others."

To cheer Harry up I said, "I'll go to see the little girl this week." What was I thinking? I hadn't even asked The Boss if she could take me. Now what was I going to do, I'd said it and I couldn't let Harry down.

"Oh, Alfie, would you? That's wonderful," he said, jotting a little note next to 'Mole's ring' on the list.

I hadn't heard Nicole come up behind me and when she put her arms around me, it quite made me jump. "Can we come too?" she asked. "I think I might be rather good at persuading a girl to return the ring."

"I shall have to go by car again," I said. "I suppose I could explain to the boss, but it's probably easier to go on my own."

"Right," said Harry still distracted. "Now, I could see this rabbit this afternoon and if I'm not too late I might be able to call in on this field mouse on my way back. Well I'd best be off." And with that he picked up his list and scurried off towards the edge of the wood.

"I wish I could be more involved," said Nicole. "It's all right for you. You went to see the dealer and now you're going to see the little girl. All I get to do is stay back here and make cups of tea. I want an adventure."

"You did have to sign the papers at the Bank," I said, trying to be helpful.

"Yes, but until we find any needy young animals, there

won't be anything else to do on that either." Nicole looked sad.

"Perhaps you could look for some needy animals. Where do you think they would be?"

She shrugged and sat down, with her head in her paws.

I hated seeing her like this and sat down next to her. "I don't know what to say," I said. "I'm not very good at this."

"At least you're here," she said putting one paw in mine and wiping away a tear with the other paw.

"I thought," I said hesitantly, "I thought you were happy. I sort of thought that you and Harry had become, well, 'a couple'"

"Good heavens," she said. "Did you? I had no idea. Oh, he's a very dear hedgehog, but I don't think we would be compatible like that. I suppose one day I'll meet another squirrel, and we'll chase through the trees together, but I don't really meet very many around here. I suppose I spend so much time with the three of you that I don't meet many of the squirrel community."

Although I felt a little sad for Nicole, I did feel quite relieved to hear that she and Harry were just friends and I snuggled just a little bit closer to her.

CHAPTER 20
THE STORY OF THE ESCAPE

The following day Harry wasn't out and about. I was just sitting with my nose pressed against his window, trying to peer in, when he threw back the curtains and got a dreadful surprise.

"Morning, Harry," I called, "I was starting to worry that you were ill. It isn't like you to be so late up in the summer."

"I'll be out in a minute," Harry called and scurried off to get himself washed. As he came out of the front door, he found Nicole had joined me and was carrying a little tray with 'just before elevenses' on it.

"Yesterday was quite a day," he said. "It makes me feel really bad when the animals tell me about the crimes I committed and what effect it had on their lives. Whereas I can only barely remember the incident at all. Take the rabbit I was telling you about." He raised his paw. "He's such a pleasant chap, and although it was only a few bits and pieces I took, nothing of any real value, he presumed he had problems with one of the young bunnies and it caused all sorts of arguments in the burrow for weeks. Most of the animals I've seen have said that if I'd told them that I was in need, they would have been only too happy to help me out. The rabbit even said he could have given me a job to help me get on my feet. The problem was I never asked. I just got on with stealing things. Then I got labelled as 'a bad lot' and no one wanted anything to do with me."

I didn't know what to say.

"It makes me realise how lucky I've been," said Nicole quietly.

"Well," said Harry, "it's no good sitting around regretting it all, I've got work to do to put it right. Have you arranged to see the little girl yet, Alfie?"

"Yes." I was relieved to have some positive news. "We can go on Wednesday."

"We?" he said. "Are we coming too?"

"No, The Boss is just taking me," I said. "But we could try to have a stowaway again. I think it would have to be Nicole or Rabbit though. I don't think you'd manage to get in or out on your own."

"Oh right," said Harry looking disappointed. "Rabbit's always looking for adventure. Take him."

"Did I hear my name?" Rabbit bounced up to join us.

"You're coming with me to see the little girl," I said grinning.

"Cool," said Rabbit bouncing round in a circle. "Are we going now?"

"I would have gone tomorrow, but with Youth Club there isn't much time."

"Wednesday it is," said Harry. "I've got more visits to do this afternoon. I want to have completed as many as possible before I see the Woodland Council on Friday. I want to be able to stand there and tell them how much progress I've made to put things right."

Tuesday all thoughts were on the Youth Club. There was the getting ready for it and then the enjoying of it. For me that was quite enough to fill the day. This week's Youth Club passed without incident and everyone had fun. The two deer were getting on fine and as promised the elder one stayed behind to clear up, to earn some money.

"You know I really can't see what it is the Woodland Council want to see Harry about. There doesn't seem to be anything we're doing wrong," I said to Nicole and she nodded.

Part way through the afternoon a helicopter went over and I remembered the day I first heard about Harry, when he'd escaped from the Woodland Prison and everyone was looking for him. I'd never asked Harry about it before, so it seemed a good opportunity.

"Harry," I said, clearing my throat nervously. "How did you escape from the Woodland Prison that time?"

Some of the other animals overheard and started joining in until they all started chanting, "Tell us the story, Harry," and he smiled with delight at being the centre of attention. He completely forgot about Friday's Woodland Council meeting and trying to make a good impression. He got all the animals that wanted to hear the story, to gather round and then he began.

"The day it happened was quite a busy one at the prison. A stoat arrived, having been arrested for vandalism and a rabbit had been transferred in from a neighbouring prison. There was so much excitement that when they let me out of my cell for exercise, no one noticed the mop and bucket left out from cleaning. Except me of course. I had noticed it. I figured that I would try to hide under the mop, inside the bucket and see where they took it. I had a bit of difficulty climbing up the bucket and it smelt of disinfectant, but it was a small price to pay for a bit of excitement. I never dreamed it would give me a way out of the prison; I thought I'd just get to see a different part of the prison and have a bit of fun. Anyway, it turned out that when they saw the bucket the warders did put it away, but the cleaning cupboard is in a little shed, just at the back of the prison and outside of the security fence. No one had ever thought it was a risk and so I got the chance to hide in the cupboard. After the warder had gone, I managed to squeeze under the bottom of the shed, by scratching away at the earth and set off as quickly as I could, which as you know isn't very quickly. As it turned out the search began quite soon afterwards. When they started returning the other animals to their cells after exercising, they very quickly spotted that I wasn't there. It's quite funny now, thinking about how shocked they must have been when I was nowhere about. I would probably have been better hiding out in the cupboard for a couple of days. It was a bit of fun and excitement and gives me a story to tell."

"How did they find you?" asked the young deer.

"Ah well that's the sad bit," said Harry laughing. I hadn't got my glasses on when I left, so my eyesight wasn't all that good. I can just about get by without them, when I know my way around, but I was feeling very anxious and not really thinking straight. I went up to ask directions from another hedgehog, thinking one of my own was less likely to turn me in, but it turned out to be a brush that one of the workmen was using. So I was found very quickly."

Harry loved every minute of the other animals asking questions about the escape, then some of the younger ones wanted to play games of hide and seek, trying to escape from their hiding places before they were caught.

Throughout the whole thing, Nicole sat quietly in the corner looking worried. Afterwards she said to me, "I hope they don't go home and tell their parents all about this evening. They might think Harry is being a bad influence. Then where will he be with the Woodland Council?"

I hadn't thought of that. I felt sheepish, as I thought about having encouraged Harry to tell the story. "You should have said something."

"How could I?" she said, "Harry was having the time of his life," and she sighed a very deep sigh.

First thing next morning I picked up the map and after some time of turning it in all directions to work out which way to walk from the park, I found it much easier to picture when I held the map upside down. I wished Nicole could go with me. I couldn't help but think that her cute looks would help in this situation. Rabbit wasn't likely to have the same effect at all.

Rabbit was ready and waiting and we managed to get him in quite easily. I looked back and could see Harry's paw waving from out of the bottom of the bush. As we drove along, I was sure I heard the sound of snoring. I prodded Rabbit and he rolled over under the blanket.

When we got to the park I created the usual diversion and waited for Rabbit to come tumbling out, except he didn't and then the door was closed and there was still no sign of Rabbit. I looked over my shoulder as we walked away and there was Rabbit with his nose pressed up against the glass, still on the inside of the car, looking forlorn. I tried to think if there was anything I could ask to go back to the car for, but there wasn't and I had no choice but to leave him there looking miserable.

The Boss agreed to let me have a run around on my own. She planned to go with me to see the little girl, but I had other ideas. As soon as I was free, I started to follow the directions I had memorised. I stopped and thought carefully about which paw was left and which was right on a couple of occasions, but it wasn't too bad. I eventually came to a road with the same name as on the paper that the dealer had given me. I then padded along the road until I found the correct house. It was a large white house, with garden around every side. There was a metal fence around the edge. It was fortunate that it was a nice day, as I had no idea what to do next. I couldn't ring the bell to ask to speak to the little girl. My best option was to sit by the fence and hope that she came out to play in the sunshine.

Fortunately, I didn't have long to wait. The girl who trotted down the steps to the garden wasn't quite as small as I'd been expecting and for a moment I worried that I might have the wrong person. I coughed a little woof to get her attention and did my best to look cute. I sat with my tail wagging, a bit like a brush moving the leaves on the ground behind me and put my head on one side with my eyes opened wide so that she could see how big and brown they were. I crossed my paws that this wouldn't be one of the types of little girls that didn't like dogs. I was in luck and she thought I was very 'sweet'. I wasn't too taken with the idea of being described as 'sweet', it didn't fit the macho image I was trying to build, but today for Harry's sake, I would overlook it. Growling would not have helped my cause. I spent some time being generally friendly and politely getting to know her before speaking.

Once the introductions were out of the way, I quietly asked, "Can you spare a few minutes to talk to me?"

As with most children, talking to animals comes naturally and she immediately said, "Yes, do you want to come into the garden?"

"I think I'd better stay out here," I replied nervously, "I can't stay long. The Boss will wonder where I've got to." I was past the stage of worrying that the little girl was about to run into the house shouting, 'I've found a talking dog'. Instead, I was worried about what I should say next. "It's a long story, I don't know where to begin."

"You could try the beginning," said the little girl and

she sat down on the grass, with her hands linked on her lap and put her head on one side to listen. Her pig-tails flopped to the side.

"Right, the beginning. But I'm not really sure where the beginning is."

"Just try," she said, "it usually works."

"Ok, once upon a time, a couple of years ago, there was a little old widowed mole who lived all on her own."

"Is this going to be like Red Riding Hood and the Wolf?" she asked excited.

"I don't know that one," I said. "Is there a hedgehog in that too?"

"A hedgehog," she said, "I thought you said a mole?"

"Well there is a mole, but there's a hedgehog too," I was getting confused.

Then I told her the story of Hedgehog's life and how he stole Mole's ring. Then I told her about the Woodland Prison and how Harry was trying to put things right. When I finished I looked up at her as best as I could and said "… and we were wondering whether you might be able to help?"

The little girl had tears in her eyes as I explained the hardships of Harry's life, before I even got as far as the dear elderly mole. When I finished she sat and thought for a few minutes and then, as though she had made a decision, she said, "Wait here," and off she ran into the house.

I wasn't sure what to do once she'd gone, so I paced up and down a bit and visited the odd lamp post and tree for a sniff, to stop me feeling conspicuous. It felt as though she was gone for ages before she came back with a little package wrapped in a handkerchief.

"Please," she said. "Give this to Harry Hedgehog, there's something in it for him too."

I was beside myself. My tail wagged and I nuzzled up to her to say the biggest thank I could possibly say. We said our goodbyes and I trotted off, carrying the little package carefully in my mouth as I went.

Fortunately, by the time I got back to the park, The Boss was still engrossed in her book and despite being disappointed that she missed the adventure, she forgave me. However, when we got back to the car and she opened the door, there was Rabbit stretched out asleep on top of my blanket.

"Alfie!" said the Boss.

"Ok, I can explain."

Rabbit opened one eye and sat up with a start. "G'day, mate," said Rabbit. "Does this mean I can sit in the front and look out of the window on the way home?"

CHAPTER 21
THE RETURN OF MOLE'S RING

The next day, Rabbit and I headed to Harry's pile of leaves, carefully carrying the little package.

Harry saw us approach. "Did you? I mean, have you? Well what I was trying to say is…"

Nicole poked her head out from inside, laughing and said, "What Harry is trying to say is, how did you get on yesterday?"

"We were awesome," said Rabbit.

"Rabbit!"

"Ok, well I would have been if I'd had the chance. But I did get to look out of the windows of the car on the way back."

"I haven't opened it, but this is the package the little girl asked me to give to you. I'm not certain whether it's the ring. She did say there was something for you," I said before Rabbit could continue.

"For me? What could be for me? If it is the ring, will you all come with me to see Mole."

"Oh yes," said Nicole. "At last I can be part of the action."

"I think you'd better open it first though, she really did say there was something for you," I said.

He took the parcel very carefully in his paws and unfolded the handkerchief that wrapped the package, then unfolded a piece of paper that was inside. There was another piece of paper, with a small lump in it, written in uneven handwriting, using crayon, was the word 'Mole', but the outer piece read as follows.

"Dear Mr Hedghog."

"Oh my," said Harry, "she's called me Mr."

"What does the rest of the note say?" I said jumping up and down.

He continued to read it out, "I am realy pleesed that you are doing so many nice things. I wood like to come and see you sumtime. Lily"

Although the spelling wasn't very good, we understood what Lily was trying to say.

"I think I might have the letter framed," he said, wiping a tear from the corner of his eye.

Friday was a very important day, with both Mole's ring and the Woodland Council.

"It's funny," Harry said to me, "I hadn't worn my suit for years and then I get to wear it twice. It's a good job it still fits," he said, pulling in his little tummy muscles.

"Do you have to wear a suit to go to the Woodland Council?" I asked.

"Well I don't know." He tried to brush the dog hairs off the sleeve. "I do think it's important to create a good impression. I don't want them to see me as some ruffian. I won't put it on until later. It isn't awfully comfortable and I don't want to look too serious when I see Mole."

We went to see if Mole was home. Nicole proudly carried the little bundle from Lily. Mole was really rather sweet and despite the fact that Harry had originally stolen a treasured possession from her, she made us feel most welcome.

Harry cleared his throat and began, "Well you remember I told you that the dealer I had sold your ring to had then sold it to a lady, who wanted it for her little girl's doll?"

"Oh yes," said Mole, "but have you found out any more?"

"Sort of," said Harry. The poor mole looked down, so he hurried his story along. "Well actually we've done better than find out some more. Alfie here," at which point I wagged my tail and knocked several things off the small table, fortunately without breaking them, "Alfie here," he repeated, "has been to talk to the girl."

This was Nicole's cue to get the little package out, but before she could, Mole was on her feet, clamping her tiny paws in front of her, saying, "What happened Alfie, what happened?"

I couldn't find any words so I looked at Nicole and she pressed the package into Mole's paws. Mole opened it, shaking. She went so slowly and took so much care that we thought we were never going to see the contents. Once she opened the paper, there in the middle, on a small piece of cotton wool, sat a tiny ring. Mole opened her mouth to speak but no words came out and she just sat down on the floor, clutching the ring, with tears streaming down her little brown face. By the time she could speak, it was to say she didn't know how she could ever thank us enough. She seemed to have completely forgotten that if Harry hadn't stolen the ring in the first place there would never have been a problem.

Then to Harry's embarrassment, she went over to him and hugged him. Well as Harry said afterwards, there aren't many people who will hug a hedgehog at the best of times, the prickles tend to put them off, but he seemed to very much appreciate it and went a funny pink colour every time we mentioned it later.

As we left Mole's house, I said, "Hadn't you ought to be getting ready for the Woodland Council?"

"I suppose so," said Harry reluctantly.

"Shall we wait for you on the edge of the wood, to find out how you get on?" asked Nicole.

"No," he said firmly. "It might be a late night, and besides, if it's bad news, I think I would like some time on my own. You can walk with me as far as the edge of the wood, when I go in, but then I'll find you in the morning when I'm ready."

We walked with Harry as far as we were allowed and then stood and watched until he was out of sight. "I suppose that's it then," I said, kicking some leaves.

"We could try to get closer," said Rabbit. "Come on."

"Sorry, Rabbit. I don't feel like an adventure. I don't want to get Harry into trouble," I said sadly.

"Oh, yes right," said Rabbit, looking down at his paws. "I'll go home then," and he bounced off.

"Yes," said Nicole. "I guess he'll find us when he's ready. You don't suppose he would just pack up and leave do you, if it's bad news?"

"I don't know. I was thinking the same thing." We arrived at Nicole's house. "Goodnight, Nicole, I suppose I'll see you in the morning."

When I arrived home, I curled up in my basket, but I couldn't get comfortable. I lay there thinking about Harry and about all the things we'd done together. How dare the Woodland Council want to stop the Youth Club?

I wasn't asleep. I was watching patterns in the shadows and starting to feel a little bit frightened on my own. I heard a tap. I jumped.

A voice whispered, "Alfie."

This time I sat up. Surely, shadows couldn't talk. I

huddled in the corner of my bed and pulled my toys and blanket towards me. I tried to curl up again, but I was too awake.

"Alfie." The tapping at the window began again.

I looked up and could see two tiny eyes peering at me. I was terrified. What should I do? It couldn't be a nightmare I was sure I was awake. I pinched myself to check and caught a rather tender bit of skin. I yelped. Then I heard the thing at the window say, "Alfie, are you all right?" Then there it was again. "Alfie, it's me Nicole." Was this real or was it all a trick. Perhaps it was a fiend pretending to be Nicole, just to make me trust it.

I sat very still and heard another voice, that I couldn't mistake, "Hey, dude."

I breathed a sigh of relief and answered them. "Hang on, I'm coming. I can't open this door; I'll come around to the front." I quietly opened the front door and sat on the doorstep until the others got there.

"Sorry to frighten you," said Harry, "but I wanted to tell you all at once, so we came to find you. We didn't like to ring the bell at night."

"That's why I climbed up the ivy," said Nicole.

"How did you get out at this time?" I asked Rabbit.

"Oh, it's easy," he said. "I do it all the time. I've dug a passage off my bedroom that Mum doesn't know about. It's covered up by a picture during the day."

"Oh forget all that," I said, jumping up and down. "What happened?"

"Well," said Harry "it isn't bad news after all. It turns out that the Woodland Councillors have been keeping an eye on me and have been delighted by what we've been doing. They now feel bad about turning down the den application and asked me to accept their apology."

I was delighted, but also a little annoyed that they apologised to Harry when it was my application. Now didn't seem the right time to say anything.

"They said that they learnt a lot from what happened to me and they would like to build a proper centre for orphaned animals and community activities in the wood. They said they would like me to run the Youth Club from there. They want to organise other activities as well. Oh yes, I was almost forgetting," said Harry grinning, "and the best bit is, that they asked if I will be the centre's manager and have a little house on site as part of the development."

"Harry, that's wonderful," said Nicole, giving him a gentle hug.

Harry was still in full flow. "There will be a dormitory for any of the animals that need a place to stay." Then as though it were an afterthought, "oh and Alfie they said they will write to you, to say that you can build your den as well."

I yelped in delight and ran around in circles chasing my tail. Then I yelped again, because I accidentally caught it.

"I need my bed now," said Harry. "There's all sorts of planning to do tomorrow. Goodnight, Alfie." And with that the three of them headed off down the garden towards the wood.

The next day, I went to see Harry and although I thought it was early, I found him already working with Nicole on the orphanage plans.

"Oh, Alfie, look at this," said Harry picking up a small frame from the table and showing me the framed letter from the little girl. "I'm going to hang it on the wall of my new house."

"New house?"

"Yes," said Harry, "as I told you last night, the

Woodland Council want me to live on site for the orphanage, when we can find somewhere to build it."

"You mean you won't be living here anymore?" The effects of the changes were just beginning to dawn on me. It was only then I started to realise that Harry would be leaving the garden. "You will still be very close won't you?" I was starting to feel quite sad, despite all the good news.

"Well that all depends. We have to find a suitable site to build the orphanage."

"Couldn't it be where we have the Youth Club now?" I asked.

"We're looking at several sites," said Nicole, pointing to a plan in front of her. "There is one in our wood, and then two just on this side of the far wood. It all depends where we can find enough space for something as large as that, without having to cut down any trees."

"But not where we hold the Youth Club," I said again.

Harry came to sit next to me. "No, Alfie, not where we hold the Youth Club. That site isn't big enough. Wherever I am, you can still spend a lot of time with me and you will have your den to look forward to."

Suddenly the den didn't seem nearly as exciting. Much as I wanted all the good things that were happening in the wood, I wanted my friends even more. I just didn't know how to tell them how I was feeling.

"You see," said Harry, turning to the plan of the woods. "There really isn't enough room where we hold the Youth Club." He pointed to a little clearing not far from the bridleway. "The size of building that the Woodland Council wants to build just won't fit there. In fact, for the size of building they have in mind, there isn't any land at all on this side of the wood. They have suggested," he said becoming quite animated, "one on the far side of this wood, just here." He pointed to a clearing that was home to some horses. "Then there are two sites in the far wood, here and here." He pointed to two more sites, across the other side of the road. "These are much bigger sites and if we choose either of those, then the whole project would be increased to include the next woodland as well as our own. What do you both think?" he asked looking up, his face glowing.

I took a deep breath. "Well, speaking for myself, I would like it if you were still in this wood. I can't see how we could be involved if it were in the other wood. Then there are all the young animals that come to Youth Club now, it would be much too dangerous for them to have to cross the main road. Even if it were the site in this wood, it's still much further away from here than I was expecting."

Nicole had gone quiet thinking. Harry looked at her for a response. She smiled and said, "I think all the sites could be good. It's important to choose the one that's right for the project and not just for us." I felt disappointed not to find support for my argument from Nicole, even though deep down I knew she was right.

"It will take some time to see all three sites," said Harry. "I think, Alfie, I will have to take you up on your suggestion of carrying me, otherwise we will be gone for a couple of days. Before we see them, I want to write out exactly what we're looking for so that we will know when we've found it. I would welcome both your ideas. Nicole your writing is much neater than mine or Alfie's please can you make some notes."

Nicole got some blank paper and a pen and sat at the table. She headed the paper "The Woodland Centre for Orphaned Animals" and carefully underlined it.

"Right," said Harry. "It needs a dormitory and a big

open room for Youth Club."

"And a kitchen and bathroom," said Nicole.

"And a house for Harry," I said, trying hard to enter into the spirit of the discussion.

"How many beds do you think the dormitory needs?" asked Nicole.

"Oh good question," said Harry.

We sat for a couple of hours noting down our ideas. Some were very sensible and others were a little more grand. "Do you think we could have an ice rink?" I asked. "I've always fancied trying ice skating."

"That one is not going on the list," said Nicole firmly.

CHAPTER 22
A DECISION FOR THE WOODLAND COUNCIL

With our list of requirements in paw, we set off to look at possible sites for the orphanage. I lay flat on the floor whilst Harry climbed on my back and then I got up as gently as I could. We set off to the first location, which was the one on the far side of our own wood.

"Steady there," called Harry, as I got into a rhythm and forgot I had a hedgehog perched on my back. "I'm going to slide off, if I'm not careful," he shouted, hanging on to a tiny handful of my fur in one paw and my collar in the other. I slowed down to keep my step more even. "I'm starting to enjoy this," he called. "You can see so much more from up here."

"You should try coming up a tree," called Nicole who was running up and down trunks and across branches.

"I don't think I'm quite ready for that. Dog riding is one thing but I'm really not sure I'm up to flying."

"Can I have a go?" called Rabbit as he bounced along behind.

We arrived at the clearing where the horses were happily grazing.

"This looks perfect," I said, without really looking. I was desperate for Harry to choose the nearest site. I wanted it to be easy to get to, so I could be part of the activities.

"We aren't going to make any decision until we've looked at all three," said Harry, sliding down my back to get a closer look. After a few minutes of scurrying round, he said "Ok, I've seen enough. Let's go to the next one." I started to walk away when a little voice shouted, "Hey, come back, you've forgotten to let me get on."

I went back for Harry. "Sorry, I forgot I was your transport." I got down as low as possible, for Harry to climb back on. Then we set off.

It took a while to get to the other wood and find the right part for the first clearing. In front of us was a wonderful, flat open space, which would be perfect to build a large centre and still have room outside. We could see where Harry's house would go and he could have a little garden all of his own. It was obviously the perfect location. I became sad and left it to Nicole to point out just how wonderful the site looked.

As we walked back, I made comments like, "Didn't you think the first one got more light?" and "Wouldn't it be better for the animals not to have to cross a road?"

When we got home, Harry climbed down from my back. Then I said quietly, "The decision is really very easy isn't it. That second site was much better than the other two. I can see that. Good luck Harry." Then I turned slowly and set off up the path.

"Alfie, come back," he called, but I carried on walking.

When I woke up, the following day, I imagined Harry putting on his suit and setting off to see the Officer of the Woodland Council. There didn't seem much point in getting up, but I decided that seeing Rabbit and Nicole would cheer me up.

I was just arriving at Rabbit's burrow when Harry come scurrying up and Nicole came down a tree to greet us both.

"I thought you two should be the first to know what I decided," he said and handed us a copy of the letter he had written to the Council. I just stood there, not coping well with my disappointment, so Nicole took the letter from Harry and opened it. She began to read it out loud;

"Dear sirs,
I would like to express my sincere thanks for your invitation to run the Woodland Community Centre and Orphanage. I will be delighted to serve the Council in this very important work.

I have taken some time to visit the three sites that you have proposed and have reached a decision on which will be the most suitable."

Nicole paused for breath. I started to walk away.

"Don't go, Alfie, please," said Harry. "I think you might like the next bit."

Nicole read on.

"Although it is clear that the sites in the far wood are larger and would be suitable to build a bigger centre, I think it is important to consider the following points.

1. The past that I want to make up for was one that was lived in this wood and it is the animals of this wood that I really want to take care of.

2. We have already started the Youth Club and it is proving very popular with the young animals of this wood. Their parents are unlikely to allow them to attend a Youth Club so far away, unaccompanied for their journeys.

3. To make this project a success, I will need the help of my dear friends Nicole and Alfie and it will not be possible for them to give this if I am too far away.

I have therefore decided that the best site for the new centre is the smaller piece of land on the far side of this wood.

Yours faithfully
Harry Hedgehog"

There was silence for a moment. "You did just hear what Nicole said didn't you?" Harry asked me.

"Do you really mean it?" I asked very quietly.

"Yes, Alfie. I mean it. I can't do this without you two."

"I didn't tell you," said Nicole, "but I decided that if it was in the far wood, I would move to live there so that I could still help."

"That doesn't change anything does it?" I asked.

"No, Alfie," he said. "I need both of you."

"And me!" said Rabbit bouncing out of a hole.

"I don't know what to say," I said. "Thank you. I promise I'll do everything I can to help. You won't regret this, Harry. But what about having a little garden round your house?"

"Alfie," said Harry "I don't need a garden. I've got a whole wood around me."

We worked on the plans for the Woodland Centre night and day.

"We need a little kitchen area," said Nicole, "and a store cupboard."

"We need enough room around the snooker table, so that the cues don't hit the walls," I said. "It's going to be strange actually being indoors."

"How many beds do you think we should have in the orphanage?" asked Harry.

And so we continued to work through all the points that needed to be included.

I couldn't imagine that life could get much better than

this, then I received another letter from the Woodland Council.

"Dear Alfie Dog," I read it out to the others.
"The Woodland Council has reconsidered your planning application for the building of a den and grant permission for this to go ahead, as long as the following conditions are met."

There then followed a number of minor points about size and building materials, none of which would be any issue at all. I ran round in circles chasing my tail as though I had only just discovered it was there. The fact that I had no money was a long way from my mind as I celebrated.

Youth Club continued as normal, with all the animals now getting excited about the building of the new centre and volunteering to do all the jobs they could possibly take on. The building contract would have to go to professional builders, but there would be decorating and furniture moving the animals could do themselves.

In the end it was Beaver Builders that were appointed to do the above ground work, but they couldn't start until the moles had dug the foundations. The beavers were not slow. "They seem to be doing a good job," said Nicole, when we went to look one afternoon.

"When's it going to be finished?" I asked.

"Well the building itself should be built in a few weeks," said Harry, "but with the inside to sort out it will be the end of July before everything is done."

"Are we having a big party for the opening?" Rabbit clapped his paws together with excitement.

"We can invite all the animals from the wood and the newspapers," I said

"Who shall we ask to open it?" asked Harry sounding serious.

We went quiet thinking of who would be best. "We could ask PC Badger," I said tentatively.

"Yes, we could," said Harry, smiling.

Within another couple of weeks the building was nearing completion and an army of young volunteers could be found clearing the undergrowth from the surrounding area and starting to tidy up a little garden. There were deer pulling wheelbarrows and rabbits digging the flower beds. Inside, a number of the others were helping to decorate some of the rooms and move the furniture and equipment into place. Harry spent his days going from room to room, checking progress. That is exactly what he was doing one day when I came running in, paws waving frantically.

As I panted for breath, I puffed "Harry... come quickly... there's a tree down in the wood and we think it's fallen on Rabbit's mum." Then I ran back outside to find other animals to help in the rescue.

Animals rushed from all around the forest to help and by the time I got back to the scene, they were already trying to move the trunk of the tree. The deer were working as a team and pulling as hard as they could. They had found some rope to wrap round the trunk and were then pulling to lift the tree. Mrs Mole was sitting by the side where Mrs Rabbit's arm stuck out from under the branches.

"She'd only gone to the post box at the end of her burrow," said Mrs Mole.

One end of the tree was over the entrance to the burrow, and from below, we could hear the muffled cries of the younger bunnies, calling for help. By this time, the paramedic stoats had arrived and put Mrs Rabbit on a stretcher to take her to the Woodland Hospital.

Rabbit who hadn't been in the burrow when it happened, came puffing up behind me. "Can you help me get my brothers and sisters out, Alfie? We can use the exit that goes into my bedroom and then call them through that way."

I had never seen him look so pale as he led me through the wood to a patch of brambles. "Please, help me get all these moved." He shouted starting to scrabble about at the undergrowth.

I used my paws to scrape away as much as I could, getting a thorn in my paw every so often and yelping in pain. Soon I could see a stone that covered a hole in the ground.

"Quick move the stone," shouted Rabbit, "I'm going in."

"Good luck," I called as he disappeared down the hole.

It took quite a long while before Rabbit came back, closely followed by another six bunnies who he carefully helped out of the hole. They were all frightened as to what would become of them while their mother was in hospital.

PC Badger cleared his throat, "Isn't this where you come in, Harry?"

"What's that?" said Harry looking confused.

"Orphans," said PC Badger in a matter of fact tone, "or at least temporarily parentless."

"Orphans," repeated Harry quietly, as though saying the word for the first time. Then he said, "Why yes, of course. You bunnies must all come back with me. You will be the first residents of the new Woodland Centre for as long as you need." The other animals around cheered. Nicole and Rabbit, who was the eldest, started to get the bunnies organised for the move.

Some of the other animals scurried back to the

Woodland Centre to finish moving the beds into position and tidying things up to make it look a bit more homely. By the time Nicole arrived with the bunnies, there were two neatly laid out dormitories with bunk beds along the walls. There were little pots of flowers around and a few of the Christmas decorations had been put up to make it all look a little more cheerful, even though it was the middle of summer.

Harry was nowhere in sight, so I went to search for him. I eventually found him at his pile of leaves in our garden.

"Well don't just stand there," he said. "Move some of these boxes for me."

"Where to?" I asked. "Shouldn't you be at the Woodland Centre?"

"Exactly, my boy, exactly. I do have to be at the Woodland Centre. I've got half a dozen bunnies to look after. I can't be coming back here at nights. Now run along with these boxes to the Woodland Centre and come back and help me carry the rest."

"Right," I said, trying to work out how many boxes I could balance. "I'll come back for that one," I said as one fell off my back. "I hope it wasn't breakable."

Harry continued to put his belongings into boxes as quickly as he could. "Must hurry, must hurry, need to take care of the bunnies," he kept saying to himself as he scurried round. It didn't take him very long to get everything ready. Then when he finally finished, he sat back on one of the boxes and looked at the pile of leaves that had been home. "I know I haven't lived here very long, but it has been a good home and a good start for my new life. I'll miss being here at the bottom of Alfie's garden."

Harry didn't know I'd been watching him. I'd come back for the next pile of boxes and was quietly standing behind him. "I'll miss you too." I said, with a tear forming in the corner of my eye. Then I quickly wiped the back of my paw across my face, sniffed and said, "Well I'd better be taking the next load," and I started to pick up the boxes.

"Thank you," said Harry putting his paw on my arm. "You know, I'll never forget what you've done for me. It was because you believed in me that I had any chance of starting a new life. None of this would have happened if it hadn't been for you. If the Council will let me, I'd like to call the Woodland Centre 'Alfie House' in honour of the dog that made it all possible."

I was speechless. I stood holding a box in my arms, with my mouth opening and closing. Once I managed to speak, I said, "That would be lovely. I'd like that, but it needed all of us to make it happen, at the end of the day it just shows what friends can do if they try."

ABOUT THE AUTHOR

Rosemary J Kind writes because she has to. You could take almost anything away from her except her pen and paper. Failing to stop after the book that everyone has in them, she has gone on to publish books in both non-fiction and fiction, the latter including novels, humour, short stories and poetry. She also regularly produces magazine articles in a number of areas and writes regularly for the dog press. Always one to spot an opportunity, she started school newspapers and went on to begin providing paid copy to her local newspaper at the age of 16.

For twenty years she followed a traditional business career, before seeing the error of her ways and leaving it all behind to pursue her writing full-time.

She spends her life discussing her plots with the characters in her head and her faithful dogs, who always put the opposing arguments when there are choices to be made.

She set up the short story download site Alfie Dog Fiction which she ran for six years. During that time it grew to become one of the largest short story download sites in the world. Her hobby is developing the Entlebucher Mountain Dog in the UK.

She started writing Alfie's Diary as an Internet blog the day Alfie arrived to live with her. Twelve years later it goes from strength to strength and has been repeatedly named as one of the top ten dog blogs in the UK.

For more details about the author please visit her website at www.rjkind.co.uk For more details about her dog then you're better visiting www.alfiedog.me.uk

Other books by the author

Alfie Dog Fiction

Taking your imagination for a walk

visit our website at
www.alfiedog.com

Join us on Facebook
http://www.facebook.com/AlfieDogLimited